Beach Club Bloodshed
A Summer Jenkins Mystery

Christine Wellert

DreamLifeBooks Publishing

Contents

Glossary of Hawaiian Words and Common Phrases

ʻāina: Land. This word is so all-encompassing though, and I love the beauty of the Hawaiian language to include so much in one little word. Aina is the living, breathing, magical world in which we are lucky enough to get to step foot on. The land is sacred to Hawaiians, and you can connect with them by showing that reverence when you are in Hawaii.

Auntie/Uncle: This term applies to basically anyone older than you, but not grandma/grandpa old. There is a deference shown to elders here in Hawaii that is absolutely beautiful to witness. I can't even tell you how many times I get called Auntie at the grocery store. Auntie and Uncles are also known to do some crazy things and are not to be trifled with. Ask me how I know...

Braddah: Bro, brother, buddy

Durian: A type of fruit grown in Hawaii that smells really bad. I haven't tried it so cannot comment on taste

Howzit: How's it going? What's up? How they hanging?

Holoholo: To cruise around. Used in other contexts it can mean joining in with someone for a leisurely experience.

Kakau tattoos: Traditional Hawaiian hand-tapped tattoos, the design of which is chosen by the artist, not the client. This is a very sacred art form and not to be taken lightly.

Kapu: Forbidden. A great offense to the people.

Keiki: Child or children, interchangeable for either depending on context it is used

King Kamehameha I: Said to be the first king to unite all of the islands and developed the first unified legal system, as well as set up trade on goods made with Europe and the United States. King Kamehameha Day is a celebrated government holiday every June 11th.

Koa wood: The Koa is a native tree with incredibly beautiful patterning when harvested and processed. Very valuable and coveted.

Kobayashi Maru: Fictional training exercise from the *Star Trek* series in which there is no correct answer. It's basically a no-win scenario.

Koehana: Ancient Hawaiian artifacts

Lanai: Hawaiian porch typically with a concrete floor next to the house, often with screens or windows. Often the word lanai is not so clearly defined and less formal, and represents an outdoor space with patio furniture.

Lei O Mano: Ancient Hawaiian weapon made with sharp shark teeth for extra pain

Lilikoi: Tropical fruit, also known as passion fruit, with a tart yet sweet flavor

Lolo: Crazy

Minnit Stop: Popular gas station/mini-mart known for their crispy chicken

Muumuu: Style of loose-fitting dress that drapes nicely and typically has a tropical pattern and bright colors

Nation of Hawaii: Native Hawaiian civil rights group fighting for autonomy on their land

Ohana: Come on–you guys have all seen *Lilo and Stitch*! Ohana means family, which includes close friends

Ono Wahine: Beautiful/desirable woman

Pau'ole: jerk or asshole

Popo: Police/Law Enforcement

Pupu: Little bites or appetizers. In true Hawaiian fashion, a pupu plate is a lot of food!

Shibari: Japanese rope art involving people being bound in certain patterns or formations, usually naked or with very little clothing. Oohh, think of the chafing...

Stink Eye: This is very universally understood and has a version in every culture. It means you're getting the "look". The look that says mama is displeased, straighten up!

Yakuza: Japanese mob

Chapter One

SUMMER

"Hey, Summer!" Brody yelled from near the bathrooms before heading towards me, flexing his chiseled abs for the girl in a yellow bikini as he walked by.

Looking up, I rolled my eyes. My guess was the toilets needed unclogging in the ladies' restroom again and Brody wanted me to take care of it. I groaned inwardly as I trudged up to the little storage shed nearby.

"This is the second time this week." I grumbled, putting my long, dishwater blonde hair up in a bun before digging around for the plunger and some gloves.

Brody patted my shoulder. "Yeah, but you know I can't go into the ladies' room. I might see something in there I can't unsee," he rationalized.

"Well, you better make sure no one drowns while I'm dealing with, well, whatever awaits me in there," I said, shivering dramatically.

"I got you, sis. You know I'm a much better lifeguard than plumber."

I hated to admit it because I was pouting about bathroom duty, but Brody was right. He was a shit plumber, but one of the best lifeguards on the whole Kona coast.

"Yeah, yeah. I hope Mrs. McMurray comes over and asks you to rub sunscreen all over her back."

"Aww, Summer, why you gotta do me dirty like that?" Brody asked, shuddering as he headed to our lifeguard station.

I walked past the beachside restaurant, Napua, that my best friend Lani worked at and glanced inside. Normally she had Sundays off, but sometimes she picked up a shift if they needed her.

I didn't see her around though, which meant I couldn't stall and complain to her about bathroom duty—again. She was probably sick of hearing it, but hey—what are best friends for?

Fifteen minutes later, after a successful fight with the antiquated plumbing, I sauntered back to the lifeguard shack where Brody sat, mirrored sunglasses reflecting the stunning turquoise waters in front of him.

Brody gave me his lady killer smile, the one that had the beach bunnies falling all over him. Too bad he was wasting his efforts on me. I knew he went after any woman with a pulse. His handsome, part-Hawaiian, part-European features and charming, devil-may-care attitude hid a heart of gold, and he was a good guy to be friends with. But if you looked up the definition of a player in the dictionary, his picture would be right there at the top.

"Hey, sis. I'm going to go on my break now, eh? A sweet little thing was giving me the eye. I gotta go share the aloha with her, Brody-style."

Groaning loudly, I made puking noises at him. Brody really was a walking boner sometimes. He grinned wolfishly at me before heading over to the Mauna Lani Excursions hut.

I'd just settled back into my lookout when I heard a shout. Scanning the ocean in front of me for the source, I saw something dark floating out way past the buoy. I lost it for a second, then noticed snorkelers waving and motioning in the same direction.

Grabbing my rescue tube, I raced to the snorkelers. Cold shocked my system as I jumped in and swam over to them.

I was in my element in the water-I'd been swimming since birth. Literally. My mom, a crystal-wearing, tarot card reading, 'make love, not war' hippie, gave birth to me in a bathtub. I've been swimming ever since.

"What's going on?" I asked the snorkelers, keeping my voice calm and reassuring.

"I think I saw a body floating by. I was afraid to get too close in case there were sharks swimming around it." The boy looked to be around fifteen, his bright sunburn giving him away as a tourist. The girl at his side, eyes wide as saucers, clung to him and looked to be on the verge of crying or freaking out.

"Okay, guys, thank you for handling this so well. Why don't you all head in and I'll take care of it."

Nodding, the boy took the girl's hand and started pulling her towards the beach.

As I got closer to the spot they'd gestured towards, I could see it was indeed a body. Swimming carefully in that direction, I called out, "My name is Summer. I'm a lifeguard and I'm here to rescue you." Once I flipped him over, though, I could tell there was no saving him. His face was blue and bloated from his time in the water, his body covered in jagged cuts.

The boy had been smart not to get near the body—the type of injuries covering it could induce a curious shark to come check it out. Humans are not generally on the menu for sharks, but they are opportunistic and have been known to scavenge in cases like this. I took a moment to scan the water underneath me, no sharks, just a few curious reef fish. *Phew.*

The body was heavy and awkward as I pulled him to shore. Brody met me part of the way in and helped me drag the body up on to the beach.

"This haole got all kinds of messed up before his swim, that's for sure."

Futilely, I checked for a pulse. "What do you mean?" I asked him as I checked the dead man's pockets for identification.

"Sis, those marks look like they're from a Lei o mano."

Looking closer, I saw what he meant. The marks were deep and jagged, though short, and spaced apart precisely, typical of a club-like weapon like the ancient Hawaiian Leo o mano, created with Kailua wood and shark teeth. On top of the lacerations, bruises covered his torso, overshadowing the bloated blue of his skin.

"Shit," I said. "You're right. I wonder if that's what killed him?"

We both looked up when we heard sirens. A crowd had gathered around us, some looking scared and solemn, others openly taking video or pictures.

I blew out a breath and shook my head. *People.*

Brody hopped up to handle crowd control while I stayed with the body. My whole body started to shake. I'd seen dead bodies before, and had taken part in hundreds of rescues, but none of them were as gruesome as this.

An ambulance pulled up and two medics jumped out, grabbing a stretcher from the back and rushing over to us. They slowed down considerably when they saw me shake my head and make a slashing motion across my neck.

"Hey, Summer."

"Hey, Mick. Good to see you," I greeted. Mick and I went way back. Both avid scuba divers, we dove with the same group at Kohala Divers as often as possible. His wife, Jenny, and he lived near my condo in Waikoloa Village.

He nodded, then asked, "So-what's the story?"

As I filled him in, I noticed the crowd growing. Following my glance, he tipped his chin and said, "Alright, let's get him loaded up. We can have the ME confirm the time of death at the hospital."

Brody came over and put his arm around my shoulder in a brotherly fashion as we watched them load up. As Mick stood at the driver's side door filling out paperwork; he called out, "Any I.D., personal items, or jewelry on him when you brought him in?"

I shook my head no. Mick saluted me, then hopped in and drove off.

"You okay, sis?" Brody asked quietly.

"Yeah, I'm alright. That was messed up, though, you know?"

He squeezed my shoulder before turning me around and leading me towards the shack. "Why don't you take a break? Go for a walk and shake it off."

"See, this is why you're not totally deplorable." I told him.

"Aww, don't get too mushy. I told Mrs. McMurray you'd help her with her sunscreen once you got back." His devilish grin turned into a squeal when I pinched his inner arm.

"You really are something, you know that, Brody?"

"That's what all the girls tell me." He laughed and jumped out of the way of my half-hearted punch.

I headed over to the nearby dock and stood at the end, wondering who the victim had pissed off. A shiver ran down my spine. I hoped I never ran into whoever did that to him.

Chapter Two
COLE

Murder wasn't something that happened often on the Big Island. Especially the type that involved the wealthy mainlanders with vacation homes in the privileged enclaves of West Hawaii.

The medical examiner had quickly ruled this death a homicide. No water in the victim's lungs meant he was dead before being dumped in the water. The lacerations and bruising on Wainright pointed to a brutal beating; his murderer had been thorough.

After identifying our victim through fingerprints, we scoured his home, looking for any clues about what or who could've caused his murder.

His home was tucked back in to a cul-de-sac overlooking the ocean on the Mauna Lani property, a haven for the millionaires and billionaires that liked to call the Big Island home, at least for part of the year. His home was furnished and decorated in that generic style that all the property owners believed to be "authentic" Hawaiiana.

Nothing stood out until we got to the kitchen/dining room combo. Broken dishes and overturned chairs, along with droplets of blood drew my attention. I asked our crime scene guys to get photos and moved on.

I poked around the rest of the house, finding a safe in a downstairs closet, the heavy wooden door slightly ajar. Inside the safe were stacks of U.S. dollars and euros. Several large gold chains and Rolex watches were perched on the middle shelf, leading me to believe this wasn't necessarily a robbery gone wrong.

Folders neatly stacked on the shelf below contained legal paperwork, including certificates of authenticity for various items and bank statements for institutions in the U.S. and abroad.

Upon closer inspection, all the jewelry in the safe had corresponding certificates; however, I found one certificate that described a rare, ancient Hawaiian artifact said to belong to King Kamehameha the First, a Lei o mano. But after a thorough search of the safe and the rest of the home, as well as Wainright's lava-orange Porsche 911 parked in the garage, the Lei o mano was nowhere to be found.

"Well, I think we have a good idea what the murder weapon was— the lacerations and punctures match." Jonah held up photos of the body and a picture he must have found online of a Lei o mano and pointed out the similarities. "Now we just need to find it, and find out who would've been angry enough at Wainright to murder him," my partner concluded. Not one to jump to conclusions without proof, I just grunted noncommittally.

At the station, I scoured the internet and Wainright's personal records, but the only clue I found was a Facebook post Wainright made alluding to attending a private, invitation-only auction on the Big Island, including a picture of Mr. Burns from *The Simpsons* cartoon, and the caption, -*'I ought to club them and eat their bones'*- with shark emojis framing the post. Rolling my eyes heavenward, I continued to search through the files and made a note to research auctions on the island.

Wainright had quite the diversified portfolio, as well as friends in high places. And upon closer inspection, some questionable associates as well. Viewing his Tinder profile, it was clear he also thought he was God's gift to women.

While I'd found some interesting information, nothing jumped out at me for enemies. He'd been divorced for twelve years, his ex-wife twenty-two years his junior. She'd received a nice payout in the divorce, but no alimony. Wainright didn't have any children of record, and his closest living relative, a distant cousin, lived in a commune in Costa Rico and told me over the phone he hadn't seen Wainright for over twenty years.

After I hung up, I leaned back in my chair, blowing out an irritated breath. So far, no one jumped out as having a motive for his murder, and as the TV show; *48 Hours*; highlighted, time was of the essence.

"Peterson!" Chief Takada yelled from across the room.

My neck tightened imperceptibly, and I inhaled, counting to ten before answering.

Turning, I asked, "What's up?"

"We just got a tip about the Wainright investigation. Anonymous caller. Said Lanikai Davis, some waitress at Napua, was seen arguing with the victim Wednesday night. We sent a patrol out to talk to her at home—neighbors say they haven't seen her. It's her day off according to the manager at Napua. I've got some calls out to family and friends but haven't heard anything back yet."

My ears perked up—this could be interesting. But when I looked around, I noticed a couple of the beat cops shift uncomfortably and go silent. *Weird.*

Chief Takada filled me in on the rest of the details from the call while I grabbed my badge and service revolver, preparing to head out and follow the lead.

"After you talk to her coworkers, I recommend you talk to the lifeguard who pulled our victim out of the water."

"I thought someone already interviewed her?" I questioned.

"The lifeguard is Lanikai Davis's best friend, according to our source." His expression was openly suspicious.

"Don't forget to check in with updates," he ordered, eyes following as I grabbed my keys and phone. I opened my mouth to protest, but then thought better of it. We'd argued about this before, and it was like talking to a brick wall. I'd been a detective for four years and didn't need a keeper. He'd only joined our unit a year ago; before that he was an assistant chief in Honolulu.

I nodded curtly, gritting my teeth hard so I didn't say anything snide. We'd heard rumors about how fast and loose he'd played in Honolulu—rumor had it he'd been asked to leave after several coworkers filed grievances against him; so his approach really rubbed me the wrong way. And it seemed he was only targeting me. I hurried out of there before I said something I might regret.

I'd just stuck the key into the ignition when I heard a tap on my window.

"What's up, Kregness?"

Officer Kregness stood at my open window; his normally sparkling brown eyes serious. He'd had been on the force almost as long as I'd been alive. HPD offered the chief's job to him when our former chief retired, but he turned them down; said he was too close to retirement to mess up a good thing. Too bad–he had more diplomacy skills and knowledge than anyone else I worked with. It didn't hurt that he was island born, able to trace his lineage all the way back to Kamehameha.

"Lanikai Davis. She's part of an *old* family, if you know what I mean. Tread carefully, and respectfully. I know that girl. If she's involved, there's a good reason."

Before I could ask him anything else, he stepped away from the car and waved me off. Mulling over his words, I drove back up the coast towards the Mauna Lani complex.

I certainly couldn't complain about the view—turquoise- blue waters and clear, sunny skies that never failed to lift my spirits. My favorite time of year were the winter months, when the Humpback whales came to give birth, mate, and play before they headed back to colder waters for the summer. It was one big party for the whales and those of us that were lucky enough to live here. They usually showed up in late December or early January, and I was looking forward to seeing them in a couple of months.

I need to get out on the boat this weekend and get in some fishing, I thought to myself. Of course, finding a murderer took precedence, but I kept hope alive I'd wrap it up by then.

I held up my badge to the camera at the gate of the Beach Club entrance and security waved me in. The grounds surrounding the restaurant and beach buzzed with activity, tourists and owners jockeying for the few cabanas still open.

Taking in the scene, it seemed unlikely Wainright was dumped on the property. Given the current and tides, his body was probably dumped somewhere north of the beach—if I had to guess probably near Puako.

"What can I get you?" the dark-haired bartender asked, brown eyes bright and welcoming.

I held up my badge. "I'm here to get information on Lanikai Davis. My understanding is that today is her day off, correct?" I asked, my tone friendly and using my most charming smile.

The bartender, Kalani, from the name on his badge, stiffened and his eyes chilled. Nodding curtly, he answered, "Yeah. She's off today." He turned his back to me and started drying glasses and hanging them up on the rack above him.

"Have you seen or heard from her today?"

He shook his head. "No."

"Do you mind if I talk to the other staff?" My tone didn't leave any room for argument.

He waved his hands in the general direction of the restaurant. "Not my call, bro, you're the boss."

I noticed curious glances from two servers standing behind a half-wall as they shined silverware. I headed in their direction but was waylaid by a tall, beefy Hawaiian man.

"Hey, boss. Can I help you with something?" he asked me, his pitch rising on the last word, his demeanor had 'manager' written all over him.

I explained who I was and why I was there. Seeming less than impressed, he pointed to the bustle in front of us.

Well, boss, my staff is balls- deep right now trying to take care of our guests. I suggest you keep your questions short if you can." Abruptly, he shifted out of the way as a server rushed by carrying two large trays of food.

The rest of my time at Napua was just as fruitless. No one had seen or heard from Lani on her day off. Knowing how close coworkers can be I asked one dishwasher if that was normal. He just shrugged his shoulders. "Lani's her own person, man. Don't mess with her, she won't mess with you."

I sent a quick text to the department to get the lifeguard's address, relieved it was only a ten-minute drive away. I hoped my interview with Summer Jenkins went better than the ones here at Napua. If not, that fishing trip might not happen 'til Christmas.

Chapter Three
SUMMER

"SO, WAIT, YOU RESCUED a dead body covered with wounds made by a Hawaiian war club? That's so cool—it's like an Indiana Jones movie or something!"

Elliot, my roommate and best friend, stood next to me in the kitchen, making dinner. The news played in the background on our TV.

"Your idea of cool is completely messed up." I told him. "It was anything but cool. Honestly, it was pretty gross. I'm just glad Laverne wasn't swimming underneath me checking things out." Laverne was the resident tiger shark in Honokohou Harbor, south of the Beach Club, near Kona.

"What do you think happened to the guy?" he asked me.

I shrugged my shoulders. "I have no idea. Whatever happened wasn't good."

We finished making dinner and took our plates and margaritas out to the lanai. We sat down just in time to catch the sunset, the dazzling cotton- candy- pink clouds spectacular as always.

After taking a minute to appreciate the view in front of us, we tore into our food like starved animals. When we finally came up for air, we looked at each other and burst out laughing.

"I guess I was hungry," I confessed. "I had no appetite for lunch after finding the body, and breakfast was a long time ago."

"Girl, same. Well, okay, I didn't have a dead body to deal with, but lord almighty, we've had some real high maintenance guests at the Fairmont over the last week. I almost wore out my Gucci loafers running around."

Elliot worked at the Fairmont Orchid, a high-end luxury resort on the Kohala Coast, arguably the most beautiful coastline in the world. The Fairmont was part of the Mauna Lani complex, which also included another oceanfront resort, aptly named the Mauna Lani Resort, as well as hundreds of posh condominiums and homes.

"Oh yeah? Who are they this time—a foreign diplomat that doesn't believe in tipping, or some member of a royal family that believes anyone without a title isn't worthy of acknowledgement?" I asked.

"You're close—a Russian oligarch and his security team. His crew has taken up the entire sixth floor wing and wants constant attention. I've had four members of the cleaning staff refuse to work there this week because the group is so demanding. It's worse than when Lovely Cuddles and her crew stayed."

"Yikes!" I said, remembering the stories Elliot told me about the famous influencer and the parties they threw and the destruction they left behind.

"What do you thi—" I started just as the doorbell rang.

When I opened the door, a tall, lean yet muscular snack of a man stood in front of me, sporting medium length sandy brown hair and a five o'clock shadow, making my little heart pitter pat. I couldn't help but notice an array of beautifully inked tattoos covering both well-defined arms, some native, and some nautical inspired designs. *Whoa, did I just get pregnant looking at this piece of cake?*

"Are you Summer Jenkins?"

I nodded, hoping I wasn't openly drooling.

"My name is Cole Peterson. I'm a detective for the Hawaii Police Department. Can I come in?" He flashed a badge while I stood there gaping until Elliot elbowed me none too subtly. I opened the door wide and ushered him in.

I noticed Elliot checking out the detective from the corner of my eye. I couldn't blame him—he was worth looking at.

"Ms. Jenkins, I understand you were involved in the rescue of Richard Wainright the Third this afternoon?"

"Is that the dead dude?" Elliot asked excitedly.

Inwardly, I rolled my eyes before nodding my head. "If you're referring to the body I pulled out of the ocean, then yes, that was me."

"I'm sorry—I'm sure that wasn't a great experience," he offered kindly, his voice and turquoise blue eyes understand-ing. I nodded again, feeling like a marionette on a string by now.

"Ms. Jenkins, did you find anything on the body?"

I shook my head no, and he continued, "The marks we found on him were not common. Had you ever seen any-thing like that before?"

"No, but my fellow lifeguard thought they looked like wounds from a Le-"

"Lei o mano!" Elliot broke in eagerly. I shot him a dirty look before turning back to Detective Yummy.

He looked at Elliot quizzically for a moment before resuming his earlier line of questioning. "Err, yes, the marks appear to be from a Hawaiian war tool. We can't officially confirm that yet, however. Summer, had you ever met our victim before?"

"I don't think so. He was bloated and blue, so I suppose it's possible I've come across him before, but not really likely. His name isn't ringing a bell, either."

He reached into his pocket and pulled out a picture with the man's name on it. The picture showed a middle-aged white guy with a puffy face and bloodshot blue eyes, and curly gray hair combed over what looked to be a bald spot.

"Are you sure you've never met this man before?" he asked, intensity in his voice.

I cocked my head at him, staring at him curiously. "Why? Should I know him?" I asked, wrinkling my brow.

"Two nights ago, someone saw your friend Lanikai Davis in the middle of a heated exchange with our victim in the Napua parking lot."

My heart stopped for a moment; concern for my friend piggy-backing on top of outrage at his implication.

"What exactly are you asking, officer?" I asked, my tone icy.

He replied, "We're just checking out all leads. A witness stated they saw Lanikai Davis waving her arms wildly and cursing at the man at approximately 9:00pm on Wednesday night."

"Did you ask her about it?"

"Unfortunately, we couldn't locate Ms. Davis. You're listed as one of her emergency contacts. It's interesting how someone saw her only a few nights before you, her best friend, found the body of the man she was arguing with." His matter-of-fact tone chilled me to the bone.

Elliot, who had been surprisingly quiet for the last two minutes, jumped in. "Hey! Are you trying to imply that Summer had anything to do with this dead guy? You are tapping on the wrong coconut, my friend. Summer would never be involved in a murder."

"Maybe not, but what about Lanikai Davis?" he asked, a hint of suspicion in his voice.

Elliot swallowed his next words, and we exchanged a glance. Lani was a firecracker—I'm fairly sure she'd never kill anyone, but her temper was notorious.

"Listen, Lani wouldn't harm a fly," I said, hoping the detective didn't catch the note of uncertainty in my voice, or the way my pitch went high on the last word.

Elliot nodded along with my statement, getting more and more animated until I reached over and pinched him furtively.

Throwing me a dirty look, he stopped his crazy nodding and stepped hard on my foot.

I saw the detective's lips twitch before he said, "I see. Well, I'd like to get a full statement from you before I leave. May I also suggest that if you *do* see your friend, you encourage her to come in for an interview."

I nodded woodenly, then answered the rest of the detective's questions, wishing this was all just a bad dream.

As I ushered him out the door, he spun around unexpectedly, my face running into his very solid chest. He grabbed my arms to steady me, and a zing of awareness ran through me. I may not like the questions he asked about Lani, but my body stood up and took notice. His hands gentled as he gripped me, and I thought I saw his pupils widen as he paused and stared at me for a long, searching moment.

"Summer, please try to persuade Lani to come in to the station if you see her. Wainright was connected to some very dangerous people, and I'd hate for her to get caught up in any of this," he implored quietly. The deep timbre of his voice echoed through my body long after he left.

Chapter Four
COLE

I DID MY BEST to set my carnal thoughts aside and focus on the job at hand, but I couldn't help but sneak a last peek at Summer before I hopped into my truck. I didn't think I'd ever seen a prettier liar in my whole life.

Well, maybe *liar* was too strong a word. But she and her friend Elliot were definitely holding something back about Lanikai Davis.

My gut told me Summer wasn't involved with Wainright's murder. Not just because I found her attractive. She was refreshingly authentic, down to the cute way she'd scrunched her nose and glared at me when I interrogated her about Lanikai. When I threw out the quasi-accusation that she might be involved, her shock and her friend Elliot's outrage went a long way in convincing me of her innocence.

The shifty way she and Elliot looked at each other when I brought up Ms. Davis's confrontation with the victim gave me the impression that she may have a reputation for being a hot-head. That, and the way Summer and Elliot both tripped over their words, trying to convince me otherwise.

Although the chief wanted an update, I didn't have much to report. I grimaced as I wound my way back down Waikoloa Road, red brake lights forming a snaking line in front of me. I turned my Spotify to Island Reggae and let the music envelop me while I thought about the investigation so far.

My phone vibrated on the seat next to me. *Ma.* Bracing myself, I closed my eyes briefly and took a deep breath. She meant well, but her frequent check-ins exasperated me.

"Hey, Ma. How are you?" I asked, tamping down the irritation I felt.

"Hi, sweetheart. I just wanted to check in. Make sure you were doing okay," she said, her tone hesitant.

My jaw tightened. *She means well, even if it drives you crazy,* I repeated to myself.

"Everything's fine. Don't feel you have to check in on me so much, Ma, I'm good."

"Can't a mother call and talk to her son when she wants?" she asked, heaping a nice little layer of guilt on top of me.

"Besides, Helen Tillman called me today and I thought you might want to hear her update on Kai."

Despite myself, my curiosity peaked.

"Okay, I'll bite. What did she have to say?"

My mom sniffed. "Hmph. I thought you might be interested."

How was it possible that at thirty-four years old, my mother could still push my buttons? The absurdity of it caused me to chuckle.

"I love you, Mom, even if you drive me crazy sometimes."

"Same, Cole, same." she replied, causing us to both laugh, breaking any residual tension.

"Believe it or not, my goal is *not* to irritate you." A brief pause ensued before she said softly, "I just know how hard you were on yourself about Jenny."

My initial instinct was to shut down. According to my therapist, however, I needed to confront uncomfortable feelings and not ignore them. *Ugh.*

Guilt washed over me as I thought about the night I got the phone call. Jenny and her mom were the first neighbors my mother had met when my she first moved to Hawaii. I'd seen Jenny here and there when I visited my mom, and my cop instincts kicked in as I watched her go from a glowing nineteen-year-old girl to a haggard skeleton of her former self in a little less than a year.

I wasn't surprised when Mom told me Jenny's mom had confided in her that Jenny was using meth and had just found out she was pregnant. She asked me if I would talk to her, try to scare her straight. Though not my style, I agreed to talk to her, offer her any resources that I knew about that could help her get clean.

When I saw Jenny in her car, belly swollen with pregnancy, I asked her if she had a minute. She hesitated briefly, her eyes darting left to right, but eventually agreed. We talked about my job, and she listened with barely contained impatience as she looked at her phone for the third time.

"Look, I know you're having trouble trying to stay clean." I handed her a brochure for a sober living complex for families. "Just take a look, it might help," I implored.

"Akoni won't go for that. He promised he's going to stop selling and get a normal job. We're going to get a place in Hilo and be a normal family," Jenny said, hope shining in her eyes.

"Akoni? Akoni Margolis?" I asked, dreading her answer. Jenny nodded.

My blood ran cold. Akoni Margolis was a notorious drug dealer in Puna, known for violence, which extended to his girlfriends if the stories were true. Looking at Jenny more closely, I saw faded bruises around her upper arms, and a bruise in the shape of a thumbprint on her neck.

"He do that to you?" I asked, pointing at the bruises.

Covering up the bruises with her hands, she shook her head, but the fear on her face said otherwise.

My hands tightened into fists and I clenched my jaw. I *deplored* abuse of any kind, but especially this. Surveying Jenny's pregnant belly and hollow eyes, I wanted to find Akoni and crack his head open myself.

I encouraged her to look into the sober living and pleaded with her to get away from Akoni. "Take my card, at least. If you need a hand, I know people that can help," I urged.

She grabbed the card out of my hand and shoved it in her purse, her phone vibrating with an incoming call. A glance at the screen told me it was Akoni.

"He gets mad if I don't answer right away. I gotta go." She sped off down the street, the last time I would see her alive.

Two months after that, Jenny delivered a baby boy, mostly being raised by her mother. Mrs. Tillman told my mom Jenny came and went at all hours, sometimes high, sometimes crashing.

Jenny called me one night, around three in the morning. By the time I woke up to the ring, the call had gone to voice-mail.

I didn't recognize the number, but I called back immediately. The phone connected, but no one said anything. Crashes and whimpers could be heard, but no one spoke. Then I heard a woman's voice, begging. "No, please. Stop. That hurts!" A scream, and then nothing.

"You fucking around with my woman? Well, you can come pick her up now, she's all yours." There was a deranged laugh, and then the line went dead.

Jenny was dead by the time I traced the call and dispatched officers in Puna. After a brief manhunt, Akoni was found, but rather than surrendering, he chose death by cop, attacking officers with a knife. His death, and Jenny's, were headline news for months afterwards.

"Kai's doing great. He's talking and walking already." My mom's voice brought me back to the present. Mrs. Tillman had officially adopted Jenny's son, and she called my mom with updates on Kai from time to time.

They'd moved to Kapaau, on the north side of the Big Island, right after Jenny's death. I always intended to go visit, but shame for the part I'd played in causing her death prevented me from reaching out.

"Cole, no one blames you for Jenny's death. You tried to help her. I know that. Helen knows that. *Everyone* knows that but you. Set this burden down- it's not yours to carry. The only person responsible for her death is Akoni."

I know my mom was trying to help, but talking about this just brought up my failure to protect Jenny. Someone vulnerable and in need of help. Normally, those feelings stayed locked up in a nice little box labeled "failure" in my head- until my mom brought it up. Looking back, I should've pushed harder, made more of an effort to talk sense into Jenny and get her to leave Akoni.

Shaking my head to dispel the emotions that welled up, I said, "Hey, I gotta go. I'm in traffic and it's getting heavier."

Mom's snort of derision said she saw right through my excuse. "What, too many goats in the road?"

Dammit, I thought, as I watched two nanny goats nibble grass on the side of the highway, the earlier traffic now cleared out.

"Someday you're going to have to let go of this idea that you are responsible for protecting anyone weaker than you. You don't have to be a superhero, Cole."

"Okay, thanks for the advice, Ma. Love you. Bye!" I hung up quickly before she could say anything else.

The rumble of my stomach as I hung up reminded me I'd missed lunch. Maybe I'd stop in at Napua again—it couldn't hurt to do a little investigating while I ate dinner, right?

Chapter Five
SUMMER

"SUMMER!" ELLIOT YELLED FROM the kitchen. "Get in here right now or I'm throwing your breakfast in the trash!"

"Uggggggghhhh," I moaned, my head throbbing, lack of sleep and too much wine catching up with me.

I'd stayed up late last night, Elliot and I trying to figure out what had happened to the dead guy, and how Lani could be involved. She'd popped off about customers before to me, but as far as I know, she'd never actually confronted one.

On top of that, it didn't sound like she and the victim ran in the same circles. Lani had about a million different cousins on the island and the same number of friends, but none that would have been involved with Wainright if I were to guess.

Once I finally made my way to bed, it was after one in the morning. Even though I was exhausted, I couldn't get my mind to shut off; worry for my friend and confusion about Wainright's murder and how Lani factored in kept me awake until well after three in the morning.

"I'm coming!" I hollered back to Elliot as I rolled out of bed and thundered into the kitchen.

Elliot handed me a cup of coffee and raised an eyebrow at me.

"What?" I said defensively. "Why are you giving me that look?"

Looking me up and down slowly before making a face, he turned back to the pan on the stove. "No reason," he said.

Instantly suspicious, I peered into the hallway mirror and winced. My dark blonde hair was a tangled bird's nest and when I looked closely, I saw the remnants of drool on my cheek.

"Yeah, yeah," I muttered.

Elliot was just a teensy bit judgmental about appearances. And when I say a teensy bit, what I mean is, he could give Anna Wintour a run for her money.

Style-wise we were the exact opposite—I preferred easy, standard beachy clothes and wore my hair either in a long braid or ponytail most days, whereas Elliot always dressed to the nines, his hair perfectly coifed and his fashion style dictated by whatever celebrity he was obsessed with at the moment. Currently, it was Nico Santos's character on *Crazy Rich Asians*; mostly because a guest at the Fairmont asked if they were related. He'd bragged about it for weeks.

"Have you heard anything from Lani?" Elliot questioned.

I shook my head. "No, but even on a normal day, she doesn't always respond right away. I'm sure she's alright, probably just out with one of her cousins hanging from a tree somewhere," I said, with more certainty than I felt. Her survival skills were legendary—her dad, a Vietnam Vet and proud conspiracy theorist, taught Lani from a young age how to survive on her own in the jungle. All she needed was an axe, a few cans of food, and her water purifier, and she could survive for weeks. The last time she'd disappeared like that was a few months ago after a particularly bad breakup—since then she'd been better at keeping her family and me in the loop if she'd be gone for more than a day or two. That, combined with the snackalicious detective's concern about the men Wainright associated with had me on edge.

I shot a text to her cousin Oliver, crossing my fingers they were just out doing tree work on their family zipline course. If I didn't hear anything from Lani or Oliver by this afternoon, I would officially be worried.

Elliot interrupted my roving thoughts. "So, what are you doing with your day off?" he asked me as I set the table.

I shrugged my shoulders, slightly frustrated with myself. Lately, I'd felt dissatisfied with certain aspects of my life. While I loved lifeguarding, I barely made enough money to get by. I thought about getting a second job waiting tables or something, but at twenty-seven it seemed like I should have more of a career path figured out.

Running my fingers through my hair, I let out a heavy sigh. "I don't know. I thought about seeing if Mauna Lani needed any part-time catering help," I said.

Elliot tsked at me as he shook his head. "Girl, you know you don't want to do that. Why are you spending your time looking at jobs you don't even want? What you *should* do is take some time to figure out what you want to do full-time and go after that. You can always work as a fill-in life-guard if you're not ready to give it up yet," Elliot said matter-of-factly.

We'd had this conversation before–I knew Elliot had a point, but I struggled with the idea of getting a "proper job" where I'd be stuck in an office building somewhere.

"Yeah, maybe you're right," I told him. We finished our breakfast together, and then Elliot headed off to work. Before he left, he admonished, "Don't forget to call your dad and wish him a happy birthday."

Elliot may have his quirks, and he might get on my nerves sometimes, but he was the most thoughtful person I knew. He always remembered birthdays and special moments. *I need to get my shit together and be better at remembering that kind of stuff.*

Checking the time, I figured my dad would've just finished his round of morning golf. He lives in Arizona, down near Scottsdale, and liked to get in an early morning round as often as possible. I dialed, secretly hoping it would go to voicemail.

"Summer!" my dad answered on the first ring with obvious delight, making me feel guilty immediately.

"Hey, Dad! I wanted to call and wish you a happy birthday. Did you get in a round of golf before going into the office?"

My dad worked as a private investigator. When I was a little kid, I didn't understand what he did exactly. We always had surveillance equipment and disguises spread throughout the house in various stages of repair or use. At first, I thought maybe he was some kind of weird clown, but after he and mom divorced, he took me along with him on some of his stakeouts when he couldn't find a babysitter. I spent most of my time bored, but I'd enjoyed bragging to my friends at school that I went on stakeouts with my dad. Not that I learned much—mostly I just read or slept.

"No, I didn't have time this morning. I'm working on a pretty hot case right now and had to do some legwork for the client." His voice turned gruff when he said, "Of course, if I had my number one private eye working with me, I'd have more free time."

I rolled my eyes; glad my dad couldn't see me. He'd wanted me to go into the family business and help him run it. I tried, but after two years of general education college classes at Arizona State, I was bored out of my skull. There was no way I could've lasted another four years to get my criminal law degree. We'd argued when I told him I was moving to Hawaii, but once my mind was made up, there was no turning back.

"Dad, I love you, and I loved being your buddy when I was little, but I just couldn't live in the desert anymore- I need to be near the ocean. You know that," I chided.

He mumbled something that sounded suspiciously like "just like your mother."

"What'd you say, Dad?"

He denied he'd said anything, and we chatted for a bit longer before hanging up. Right before we ended the conversation, he told me he was thinking of coming out to visit soon.

I played it cool, but secretly I was shocked. I'd moved seven years ago and he hadn't visited me once. He refused to come visit since my mom also lived on the Big Island, albeit on the Hilo side.

Whenever I brought it up, he'd say he didn't think the island was big enough for the both of them and didn't want to risk running into her.

Heaving an enormous sigh, I hung up, relieved to check that off the list.

Feeling a little at loose ends, I looked around the condo. *Alright Summer, time to get your shit together and figure out what you want to do when you grow up.*

My phone chimed. Oliver replied to my text and said he hadn't seen Lani for a few days but heard "the Man" was looking for her and that he'd let her know I was looking for her if he saw her.

My anxiety ratcheted up. Lani *always* let Oliver know where she was. I could think of only two options: either she took off when she heard HPD was after her; or she was shacking up with the new bartender at Napua and had turned her phone off so we didn't give her any shit.

I blew out a big, gusty breath; I knew what I needed to do and who I needed to talk to. I just didn't want to do it. Picking up my phone again, I dialed about the last person on Earth I felt like talking to.

Chapter Six
COLE

"WHAT'LL YOU HAVE, BOSS?" the bartender from earlier asked as I took a seat at the bar.

"Do you have any IPA's on tap?" I asked.

The bartender nodded, his face a mask. Locals protected their own around here, and I realized I'd really bungled it earlier when I'd asked about Lani Davis. Maybe a more subtle approach would be a bit more effective in gathering information.

"Rumor has it Napua has the best food on this side of the island. Mind if I take a look at the menu?" The bartender, Kalani, handed me a menu without a word, then crossed his arms across his chest, leaving no room for doubt I'd need to work extra hard to gain his trust.

After studying the menu, I set it down and gave my order, the reticent bartender barely nodded in acknowledgement.

The last rays of the sun disappeared into the horizon as I gazed out at the azure blue ocean in front of me and felt my shoulders relax. I took a minute to appreciate my good fortune in living on the Big Island. Even with the challenges that come with living on an island in the middle of the Pacific Ocean, I loved being here.

A tall, long-haired brunette server dropped off a plate of food with a brief "enjoy," and practically threw some silverware on the counter before spinning around and marching back the way she came. My status here was persona non grata, apparently. Shrugging my shoulders, I dug in, only coming up for air after my plate was almost cleared of food.

Looking up, I noticed the bartender watching me. I gestured down to my empty plate. "They were right—best food on the island." He nodded sharply, but I noticed his posture relaxed slightly.

"Listen, I know we got off on the wrong foot. I'm just trying to do my job. We received a tip that Ms. Davis was seen arguing with the victim a few nights ago. That may or may not be related to his death, but my job is to follow up on any leads. I'd like to interview her and clear her name if possible. She has plenty of staunch allies in her corner, but rest assured all I want to do is talk to her," I reasoned.

"Boss, Lani may be many things, but she's not a killer. Of hearts, maybe, but that's about it," he said morosely.

Changing gears, I decided to ask about the victim. "Do you remember the victim, Richard Wainright? According to his credit card, he ate here several times in the last couple of weeks."

Kalani nodded. "Yeah, I remember him. Typical blowhard, bragging about this or that. He'd come and sit at the bar and talk. I didn't care for the guy. Lot of money, but never tipped worth shit. Always hitting on the staff."

"He ever cross a line? Get handsy with anyone?" I asked.

"No, we'd have shut him down and escorted him out if that ever happened. We're all ohana here, no one gets messed with and gets away with it."

"Do you think he went after Lani and she chewed him out in the parking lot?" I questioned.

Kalani shook his head emphatically. "Lani wasn't the type anyone messed with. She's tough, and anyone that has spent time around her knows right away not to hassle her. Wainright was a jerk, but he didn't come across as stupid."

I took a moment to think about Kalani's words. If he wasn't harassing her, then what had caused Lani to argue with Wainright?

Setting that aside for a moment, I moved on. "Did Wainright brag about anything in particular that you can remember?"

"Well, he talked a lot about going to some big, fancy, hush-hush auction. When I asked him about it, he acted really cagey. Just said something about how he already had the key, and now he just needed the club."

"Hmm. Do you know what he meant by any of that?" I asked.

"No, but I got the sense that the items up for auction were of the black market variety."

"Any idea what the items were?"

Kalani stopped drying the glass in his hand for a moment and seemed to think about my question before answering. "I can't say for sure. He talked about ancient artifacts from the islands a few times. He wore this necklace, a shark tooth pendant with a stone of some sort in the middle that looked pretty old. I asked him about it once. He said something about it holding the key to his power or some weird shit like that. I don't know, he was one of those haoles that come in and buy up property here and then pretend they're local, trying to fit in with Kama'aina."

I nodded my head in understanding. The Native Hawaiian culture had been subverted for hundreds of years, and the Hawaiians, rightfully, took issue with people moving in and calling themselves locals without actually contributing to the island or its people.

"Strange. Any idea if the key he alluded to was the pendant he wore?"

Kalani slouched against the counter behind him and seemed to consider my question. Eventually he shrugged. "Maybe? I guess that makes sense—he had it on every time I saw him and he was always grabbing it, almost like he was checking to make sure it was still there."

I reached out to shake his hand. "Thanks for the info, it helps me get a better picture of who this guy was and who might have beef with him." I handed him my business card and asked him to call me if he remembered anything else.

Kalani just nodded, but after I paid my bill and stood up to leave, he said, "Look, I don't know what happened to Wainright, but I can tell you this—Lani had nothing to do with it. You're wasting your time trying to find her—that girl can disappear better than anyone on this island if she doesn't want to be found."

Nodding curtly, I headed to my truck, processing all I'd learned. I tried to put all the pieces of the puzzle together that I had so far, but nothing seemed to add up. Rich dead guy who ran with high rollers, a blowhard, and Kalani had also mentioned that auction—the second time it came up in my investigation.

Now that I thought about it, the only missing item in the safe was the Lei o mano, and Kalani said Wainright had mentioned something about a club. But what was the significance of the weapon? Why would someone be willing to kill to get it? And what did Wainright mean when he said he already had the key?

Chapter Seven
SUMMER

"Thank you for calling Mauna Lani Resort Services. This is Jessica. How may I help you?" a smooth, sultry voice recited.

Grr. Even the sound of her voice drove me crazy. *I bet she practices it in front of the mirror with her best slutty smile thrown in for extra effect.*

"Hey, Jessica. It's Summer. Sorry to bother you at work, but I'm looking for Lani. Have you seen her?" I got straight to the business at hand. The less time spent talking to her, the better.

"Summer. Why do you think I know where Lani is?" Her voice took on a more normal, albeit snotty, tone. "I'm at work. Call Oliver."

I swallowed my pride before I responded. "I just heard from him; he doesn't know where she is either," I said through gritted teeth, doing my best to keep my temper at bay.

"Oh, hang on. I have another call coming in," she said in a syrupy sweet voice.

In the five minutes I waited for her to come back on the line, I had time to come up with a laundry list of reasons I hated her.

First, she'd stolen my boyfriend seven years ago by lying to him and telling him she saw me making out with his best friend. While losing the boyfriend was not a big deal, throwing shade on my reputation *was* a big deal.

After that, she'd pulled all kinds of mean girl pranks on me; from telling people I gave said ex-boyfriend herpes (I didn't) to accusing me of sharing unflattering pictures of her on an anonymous Instagram page (I might know something about that).

When I looked back over the years, I realized how dumb we both behaved. But just as I thought maybe I could let it go and start over, she'd do something else to mess with me.

I checked the time again and fumed. She definitely wanted to inconvenience me for her own enjoyment. I thought about hanging up, but worry for Lani kept me on the line.

When Jessica finally came back on the line, she merely reiterated she hadn't heard from Lani and suggested I call Uncle Raymond, Lani and Jessica's uncle in Hilo.

"Let me know if you hear from her, yeah?" she asked, worry coloring her tone. As much as we disliked each other, we both loved Lani.

Officially worried now, I texted Elliot to update him and let him know my plan to head to Hilo and follow up with Uncle Raymond to see if he knew anything about where she'd gone.

I stopped at Surf Camp Coffee, my favorite coffee shop in Waimea, and grabbed a mocha and muffin for the drive.

While I waited in line, I overheard people talking about the dead guy. Speculation ran rampant, but the consensus was he tangled with the wrong Hawaiian and got taken care of, local style.

My anxiety level went through the roof–if Lani was involved, she could be in big trouble.

Normally, I drove to Hilo over Saddle Road, past the Mauna Kea observatory turn off, but today I took the scenic route, in the hopes the ocean views would soothe my worry.

By the time I arrived at Uncle Raymond's plantation-style home, though, I was a bundle of nerves.

"Eh, girl. What you doin' here?" Uncle Raymond, his aloha shirt stretching the buttons around his massive torso, his muscular arms the size of tree trunks, called down to me from his perch on the front lanai.

He grabbed me in a breath–stealing hug, then held me two inches off the ground before gently setting me down. Tears welled up almost instantly at the kindness in his eyes as he looked at me.

"Eh now, why you leaking like that?" he questioned, his deep voice full of compassion, and maybe a tinge of alarm.

Trying to pull myself together, I told Uncle Raymond the entire story, my voice catching as I finished. "I'm worried that Lani got caught up in something and is in way over her head. The detective said there's some dangerous men involved with the victim. I don't want her to get hurt."

After my meltdown in his enormous arms, he looked at me, his normally cheerful, smiling eyes concerned.

He offered me a glass of lemonade, but knowing his propensity for spiking it with a little Kuleana rum in the afternoon, I declined.

Pointing to a seat at the patio table, he said, "It sounds like our girl made a smart decision to disappear. Maybe she saw something that puts her at risk. If I hear from her, I'll let you know." His tone held a note of something I couldn't define, and my neck prickled. Lani had an extensive network of friends and family on the island—there would be no shortage of people willing to hide her if necessary.

With a lump in my throat, I nodded. Uncle Raymond must've sensed my dejection. He reached over to lift my chin up and look into my eyes. "She's okay, Summer. I promise you that."

I sensed he knew more than he let on, but rather than press him, I let it go. If I had any chance of finding Lani, it was best to send out the message subtly. Otherwise, I risked offending her ohana and getting stonewalled.

Knowing Uncle Raymond wasn't going to share anything more with me, I got up to leave, thanking him for his time. As I opened my car door, I called back to him, "If you do hear from her, please tell her to be careful."

He waved at me as I drove away.

If I hadn't noticed Uncle Raymond go perfectly still for a moment, I almost would've missed the late model black Escalade on my tail. No vehicles drove down this far on the dead-end road unless Uncle Raymond was acquainted with them.

As I examined the Escalade in my rear-view mirror, I could just make out a partial plate, RA7, before I turned onto Hawaii Belt Road and hit the gas.

Thanks to all the years of watching too many *Fast and Furious* movies, I had a few tricks up my sleeve to turn this to my advantage. Checking to make sure they weren't behind me, I spun into a pull off hidden by giant Monstera bushes and waited.

Soon afterwards, the Escalade drove by slowly. I let another car pass before turning back on to the highway. I didn't know for sure if they were following me, but figured I'd try to beat them at their own game.

Winding back along the coastal highway towards Waimea, I thought about my visit with Uncle Raymond. If anyone could keep Lani safe, it would be him. I just hoped it didn't also put him in jeopardy.

The car between me and the Escalade suddenly slammed on their brakes, startling me out of my reverie. Looking up, I could see the Escalade had abruptly pulled over on the side of the road.

Too late to do anything but drive by, I strained to get the last three digits on the license plate. 609. I committed it to memory as I passed them.

The tinted windows made it hard to see anyone inside. I consoled myself with the fact that I'd gotten a full license plate number, at least.

Nervously, I looked in my rearview mirror, watching as they pulled back on to the highway, leaving two cars between us.

Maybe I'm just being paranoid. All the years with my dad on stakeouts, and now Lani going missing is probably just making me a little crazy.

Bam! My car lurched and my neck snapped forwards, as the Escalade ran into my rear bumper. *Shit.*

My car edged close to the guardrail over the Honoli'i Bridge. Doing my best to counter-steer against the push of the Escalade, I just barely kept it on pavement. Screeching metal against metal let me know how close I'd come to plunging two hundred feet to the ocean below.

Shaken and pissed off, I pulled over on the side of the road, hoping to confront the driver. Probably not the smartest thing to do, but my temper got the better of me.

The Escalade, however, didn't stop. I watched as it quickly disappeared around the curve; I wasn't sure if I should be grateful for that or not.

A sweet Filipino lady parked behind my car and came over to give me her name in case I needed any witnesses. She'd been behind the Escalade and witnessed the whole thing.

"Those tourists think they own the road, yeah?" she asked, flipping her wavy hair behind her. "More money than brains, most of them. Tinted windows and fancy rims like they're someone important. Meh." She sniffed in disgust, making a shooing motion with her hands towards the ocean.

I laughed half-heartedly, then thanked her profusely before I circled my car to check the damage.

Not pretty to begin with, my tan Honda now sported a caved-in rear bumper and a long scrape along the passenger side. I checked my phone. *Dead.*

Son of a bitch. My lifeguard job didn't pay the greatest, and car repairs were not in my budget. Letting loose a gigantic sigh, I hopped back into my car, thanking any entity that would listen that it still ran. I waited for the shaking to subside and my heartbeat to settle down before getting back on the road.

I drove home slowly, searching every pull off I drove past for the Escalade. By the time I got home, I was so nervous that tequila seemed like a good dinner option.

"Hey, Summer."

"Ahhhhhh!" I hollered and punched out blindly, connecting with solid flesh.

Chapter Eight
SUMMER

DETECTIVE DADDY STOOD IN front of me, holding my wrist carefully in his hand.

"I'm sorry, I didn't mean to scare you," he said, lips twitching.

"You scared me to death, especially after the day I just had!" I complained.

Seemingly mesmerized by my wrist he stared down at it for a moment before his eyes snapped up.

"What kind of day did you have, exactly?" he questioned, curious. The smell of his aftershave wafted towards me.

Warmth spread throughout my whole body, and my mouth went dry. I inched closer to him before realizing what I was doing and snatching my wrist back.

My other hand closed over the spot where he rubbed, as if to prolong the sensation.

"Summer?"

Snapping to attention, I asked him to repeat the question and then told him about the black Escalade.

"Why didn't you call the police and report it immediately?" he asked, judgement in his tone.

I held up my cell phone. "It died before I had service again."

He just nodded, then asked, "Do you think they followed you because of what happened yesterday?"

I shrugged. "I'm not sure. It's possible I overreacted and they were just careless drivers who happened to be on a desolate, dead-end road and happened to be behind me all the way from Hilo."

"Hmm." He grunted, then asked me to recite the license plate, writing it down in a little notebook.

"I'll check it out. I'm not a big believer in coincidence. We gathered more intel on Wainright today, and the people he associated with aren't exactly church goers. If you see Lani, encourage her to come forward with any information. I don't know if she's involved with his murder, but it would be better for her to turn herself in to protective custody than take her chances with Wainright's business associates."

His words chilled me to the bone. Next to Elliot, Lani was my favorite person on Earth.

"Summer." Detective Peterson tilted my chin up, locking eyes with me. "Please be safe," he urged.

He pressed something into my hand and then leaned forward and murmured, "Call me if you need anything."

"Wait, why did you stop by?" I called.

He turned and looked at me for a second before walking back. "Two reasons. I wanted to ask—when you found Wainright's body, was he wearing any jewelry?"

"No. He wore a blue Hawaiian shirt and a pair of khaki shorts, that's it. No shoes, no jewelry."

"You're sure?" he asked intently.

I nodded. "Yeah, I'm sure. What was the second thing?"

"Hmm? Oh–" He hesitated, then said, "Nothing, never mind. It wasn't that important."

Intrigued, I wanted to press him for more, but he mumbled a quick goodbye and spun around towards the parking lot.

I watched him saunter out to his truck, stopping on his way to look at the damage to my car, shaking his head.

He caught me watching him, then glanced at the car. He mouthed, "Be careful." All traces of humor wiped clean.

Turning to let myself into the condo, I noticed Elliot's face pressed against the window, a smirk on his face. He mimicked fanning himself, causing me to laugh, despite myself.

"Gurrrrllllll, yes," he said when I walked through the door.

My ears felt hot, and I couldn't look Elliot in the face. Detective Peterson was a snack, and my hormones were still on high alert after our encounter.

"I'm going to go change," I mumble before racing to my bedroom and slamming the door shut, leaning against it for support, Elliot's laughter ringing in my ears.

When I finally worked up enough nerve to face Elliot, I came out and sheepishly offered to help with dinner. He smiled knowingly, but just handed me a peeler and a bowl of sweet potatoes.

"How did your visit to Uncle Raymond go?" Elliot asked as we put the finishing touches on our pulled pork bowls.

My stomach dropped as I thought about the drive back from Hilo. I filled Elliot in, surprised at his reaction when it came.

"Jesus, Summer!" He pounded his fist on the counter before he grabbed me in a fierce hug and then released me.

Elliot wondered aloud if the Escalade followed me because of Lani. I wondered the same thing.

We brainstormed and speculated on what was going on. The more tequila we drank, the crazier our theories became.

"The FBI had Wainright killed because he had information that confirmed, once and for all, that Area 51 is a bastion of alien activity and experimentation," Elliot declared just as the doorbell rang; his gesticulations wild.

Avoiding his finger as it jabbed the air, I went to answer the door.

When I opened it, though, all I saw was an envelope laying on our welcome mat.

Frowning, I scanned the area around the condo complex before I opened the envelope.

Today was a warning. You have two days to hand over the pendant before we come and take it ourselves. Leave it at Kawaihae Harbor South, Slip #2 by Saturday, we won't be so gentle if we have to ask again.

My hand shook as I set the letter down on the kitchen counter, recoiling as if it were a rattlesnake poised to strike.

Elliot, eyes wide at my reaction, picked up the letter, lips moving as he read it before he gripped my shoulders and looked at me, eyes narrowed in concern.

"Time for you to call Detective Peterson. This isn't funny anymore."

Chapter Nine
SUMMER

My hands shook a little as I punched in the number on the card Cole handed me earlier.

He picked up on the first ring. "Hello?" His deep, gravelly voice caused all kinds of parts of me to stand up and take notice.

"Cole? I mean Detective ... umm Peterson?" I babbled.

"Summer. I didn't think you'd call so soon," he said, his tone warm.

"Umm, yeah. Well, sorry to bug you. After you left, someone left a note at the front door." I read him the note.

"I'll be right over," he replied grimly. "And Summer? Make sure you keep your door locked until I get there."

"Duh." I said brilliantly, the tequila still fighting my brain cells for dominance.

"Hmph," was his only reply before hanging up.

Elliot and I waited, pacing back and forth across the condo until we heard a knock on the door. Elliot beat me to the door and elbowed me out of the way to peer through the peephole before letting Detective Da—, ahem... Cole that is, in.

He seemed to take in the condo all at once, his shoulders relaxing slightly before he asked to see the note. Elliot gestured to the counter where it lay.

He pulled out a pair of gloves from his back pocket and picked it up, studying it intently before turning his gaze to me.

The tequila buzz wore off with surprising quickness after seeing the serious look on Cole's face.

His penetrating gaze unnerved me when he asked, "Do you know what pendant they're talking about?"

My mind raced as I shook my head. My only guess is it had something to do with the Wainright murder. What didn't make sense is how or why I was being targeted?

"No idea. Nothing like this has ever happened to me before. Do you think this has anything to do with the dead guy?" I asked, knowing the answer even before he spoke.

Cole took a moment before he answered. "I think it's possible. Again, I don't believe in coincidences. First you pull Wainright's body out of the water, then you get run off the road, and now you're being threatened. Are they connected? I can't say for sure, but I think it's definitely worth considering. You never said what you were doing in Hilo—could that have something to do with all of this?"

My eyes darted over to Elliot, and I licked my lips nervously. If Lani *was* involved, I didn't want to lead the cops to her.

"No, I don't think so. I went to go visit Uncle Raymond. He's a family friend." I squeaked out, the pitch of my voice shrill. Elliot was nodding his head, marionette-style, halting when he caught the glare I sent his way.

"Hmm. Okay. I might need to contact Uncle Raymond to ask him some questions. I'll need his contact information."

"Umm, well, he doesn't have a phone and he's really hard to get a hold of and you just never know if he's going to be home or not." I blabbered, crossing my fingers behind my back and silently praying Cole dropped the subject.

"I see. For now, I'll leave it be, but we're going to circle back to this soon," he warned.

Gulping audibly and nodding my head, I tried to distract him by asking about the letter.

"I'm going to take this in to check for fingerprints, but my guess is yours are the only ones on here. I think that whoever was behind the Escalade rear-ending you and the note have experience keeping their hands clean."

He asked to take a look around to make sure our apartment was secure. Relieved he didn't ask any more questions about Uncle Raymond, I readily agreed. He prowled around the condo, checking the windows and door to the lanai, both inside and out.

"Bedrooms are upstairs, I'm assuming?"

Elliot nodded and asked if the detective wanted to check them out. I watched them walk up the stairs, then had a moment of panic realizing the detective was going to see my underwear laying on the floor.

Crap. I chased after them, relieved they went to Elliot's room first. I had just enough time to throw the blanket across my bed and shove most of my clothes and underwear into a drawer when they walked in.

Detective Daddy's grin told me he knew exactly what I was up to, but he made no comment, instead heading straight to the window to check it. He seemed satisfied with what he saw, and we all tromped back downstairs.

"Until we know who's behind these threats, I want to encourage you both to be extremely cautious. Let someone know where you're going and when to expect you back. Check the surrounding area when you go out to your cars and lock your doors and windows at night."

"You mean like situational awareness?" Elliot chimed in, looking proud of himself.

I snorted, and he shot me a dirty look.

"Exactly. If anything at all feels off to you, call me right away, okay?"

"Thank you for coming over tonight, detective. I'm sure you have better things to do than this," I said.

"It's my job," he said simply. "And please, call me Cole."

I followed him to the door and said goodnight. He leaned in, crowding me against the door, and murmured, "Please take care of yourself. I'd hate to see anything happen to you."

My breath quickened. I leaned towards him, his scent a mix of cedar and cinnamon. Elliot cleared his throat behind us, and we jumped apart like two guilty kids. Cole looked down and gave me a lopsided grin and saluted Elliot before he got into his dark gray Tundra and drove out of the parking lot.

"Shut it," I said to Elliot, glaring at him as I walked past his smirking face into the condo.

He mimicked zipping his lips, but I knew I'd hear about this later.

Chapter Ten
SUMMER

THE INSISTENT BUZZING OF my alarm drew me out of a graphic dream involving me and Cole on a deserted island. As my dream faded, I jumped out of bed and went to the bathroom for a quick shower to wake myself up before work.

My head was on a swivel as I checked the parking lot carefully before heading out to my car. The damage looked even worse today, and I mourned the fact that it would take months before I could get it repaired.

My drive was uneventful thankfully; just goats and other commuters on the road. Cruising through the Mauna Lani entrance I held up my pass to the badge scanner and made sure no one followed me in.

Worst-case scenarios had played out in my mind on the entire drive to work, and I wondered if this would be my new normal. My stomach roiled. I hadn't eaten anything for breakfast, worry about Lani causing me to lose my appetite. I caught myself biting my nails as I scanned the ocean on my trek to the lifeguard station and quickly dropped my hand down at my side.

"Hey, howzit, Summer?" Brody called out to me as he unfurled the lifeguard flag and planted it in front of the hut.

I quickly joined him in getting the day's opening chores done. Between the two of us, Brody and I made quick work of it. Having worked the same shift for several years, we had a good routine in place, and the daily repetition helped center me, especially today.

The morning passed quickly and by the time lunch rolled around, I'd allowed myself to relax slightly. Just as I stood up to take a break, a teenage girl, sunburn coating every inch of her that wasn't covered by her bikini, came to the shack.

"Umm, some weird old lady in the bathroom told me to let you know the toilet is plugged up and leaking on the floor."

Brody snickered in the seat next to me, and I fought the urge to smack him.

"Okay, thanks for letting me know. I'll take care of it." I told the girl.

Grabbing all the tools I needed, I headed into the bathroom, muttering curse words under my breath the whole way.

I expected to see a puddle on the floor by the door, but the floor looked dry. Shrugging my shoulders, I stepped into the handicapped stall, the usual culprit.

The door stuck, and I had to give it a little extra push to open it.

"Oomph," someone muttered from behind the door.

"Oh, sorry," I said, already backing out when a hand snaked out and forcibly pulled me inside the stall.

Spinning around, I took up a defensive position before I realized my attacker was a short little old lady, gray hair piled up haphazardly under a sunhat. Her muumuu swallowed her up, the hemline just skimming the top of her socks, which she wore with a worn-out pair of flip-flops.

Something about the old lady struck me, but I couldn't put my finger on it. Scanning her from head to toe, my eyes caught on the gold necklace around her neck with a black pearl nestled in the setting.

"Lan—" I burst out, but she covered my mouth before I could finish.

"Shhh!" she said, her eyes serious as they looked into mine.

I hugged her tightly, grateful to see her with my own eyes.

"Where have you been? I've been worried sick about you!" I whispered.

"I'm okay, but I can't stay here for long. People are looking for me. Tonight, I'll sneak into your condo. Leave your bedroom window open a crack."

Before I could ask any more questions, she was gone.

The rest of my shift passed by in a blur. No one needed rescued, thankfully, since I couldn't think straight after seeing Lani.

Elliot called me on my way home and I told him what had happened. We both raced home and discussed Lani's cryptic message and visit at length, keeping our voices low.

"Do you think she knows what happened to that Wainright guy?" Elliot asked.

Shrugging my shoulders, I replied, "I don't know. She just said someone was after her. If it was the cops, I don't think she'd be so covert."

Nervous, we both took turns looking out of the window and pacing as we waited for any sign of Lani. By eleven, I had about given up on Lani coming when she strolled down the stairs, looking normal as ever.

"You left your window unlocked." Lani smirked at Elliot. "Nice magazine by the way."

Elliot glared at her before we both jumped on her, smothering her in hugs, all of us laughing, relieved Lani was safe, and we were all together.

Lani snuggled in on the couch and we fed her leftovers. Once she finished eating a second helping and started scrounging for dessert, I decided it was time for her to answer some questions.

"So spill. What happened Tuesday night, and why are you hiding out?" I demanded.

With a last, regretful look in the fridge, she sat down at the counter and blew out a big breath.

"That okole Wainright bragged to everyone at the bar that he had one of our Koehana from King Kamehameha I. I confronted him in the parking lot and told him the Moke would come after him if he didn't return it. He just laughed in my face, that loco suckah."

Elliot and I shifted uncomfortably. We knew Lani and her infamous temper wouldn't take kindly to being laughed at.

"So, I followed him back to his house and hid in the shadows. I just wanted to get the Lei o mano back, I swear.

I parked down the road and slipped through the backyard next to his house until I saw him turn the light on in the kitchen. He wasn't alone. There were two dudes crowding around him and waving their arms. I didn't hear all the conversation, but it sounded like they also wanted the Lei o mano."

She told paused and took a big gulp of her cocktail before continuing. "Two men forced him to take the Lei o mano out of the safe, but, instead of taking it and leaving, they also dragged Wainright out to their vehicle and started thrashing him with it." She shuddered.

"I noticed the guy who was doing the beating tossed the Lei o mano onto the ground near the bushes I was hiding behind, so when they were busy throwing Wainright into the SUV I snatched it.

"I ran as fast as I could to my car and booked it out of there. I don't know if they actually saw my face, but I'm pretty sure they followed me. I lost them by Hawi, but if they took down my license and had connections, they'd be able to find me pretty easy. Uncle's been hiding me ever since."

"Jesus, Lani!" I couldn't believe all she had been through in a short time. Giving her a big hug, I told her as much.

"I'm just glad Pops is on the mainland for the next couple weeks," she said, clinging to my hand, unusual for my independent friend.

"I had a little excitement myself," I started, then told her about being run off the road. "We should stick together. Stay here with us and we can figure this out," I encouraged.

Lani shook her head. "Can't sis. You're already on their radar. I won't put you in any more danger than you already are."

We told her about Detective Peterson's, Cole, that is, visit and I said, "He seems legit, Lani. If you told him everything you know, maybe he could help."

"No way. Not only did I witness a potential murder, my fingerprints are all over the murder weapon. And I'm not giving up the Lei o mano. It belongs to my people, not to the haoles coming to the island trying to buy up our culture. If I give it back, some different suckah is just going to come on the island and hide it in their mansion. Not happening."

Lani had a point. Rich people from all over the world came to Hawaii and bought rare Hawaiian artifacts that were likely stolen from the Hawaiian people during colonization. They stored these artifacts in fancy mansions with gated access, keeping them away from the people to whom they inherently belonged.

While I agreed with the sentiment and reasoning, I feared Lani would be in constant danger until she came clean. From the obstinate look on her face, though, I didn't think that would happen anytime soon.

Chapter Eleven
SUMMER

We talked late into the night, trying to come up with ideas that could get Lani off the hook with HPD and also get the killers off Lani's trail.

By two in the morning, my eyelids were drooping more than they were staying open, so we decided to circle back in the morning.

"One thing I can't figure out though—why mess with Summer?" Elliot asked.

My hand stilled on the railing. I hadn't thought about that. Why *were* they following me?

That question haunted me the rest of the night, and when I finally drifted off to sleep, I dreamed about being chased by an unseen hand wielding a Lei o mano.

Morning came quickly, and with it, the realization that despite harboring a fugitive, being followed by murderers, and fighting my growing attraction to a hot cop, I still needed to go to work and pay bills.

Dragging myself downstairs, Elliot stood at the kitchen counter pouring pancake batter onto the griddle.

"You're a god, and if you weren't gay, I would marry you and have your babies." I declared.

A throat cleared from the living room alcove. I whipped my head around, and Cole stood next to the bookshelf, a bemused smile on his face.

"Shit." I muttered under my breath.

Elliot laughed at me silently, and I turned in his direction. "Never mind. I take it back." I told him, annoyed.

"Cole stopped by to give us an update on the Escalade that rear-ended you yesterday," Elliot relayed.

I did my best to smooth my hair back, a futile struggle considering the tangled nest it normally was in the mornings. I turned and raised my eyebrows at Cole, waiting to hear what he found out.

He cleared his throat, mirth still evident in the wide grin on his face.

"The Escalade belongs to a Japanese corporation with ties to the Yamaguchi-Gumi, a known faction of the Yakuza. I've put some pressure on the executive team of Ichiban corporation to find out who was driving the vehicle, but so far they're denying the Escalade ever went off property."

He stopped and looked at both Elliot and me, unsmiling, and seemed to choose his next words carefully.

"Normally, I wouldn't share any of this information with you. However, because you were already involved in an accident, I believe it's important for you to know what's going on."

I swallowed. I could tell I wouldn't like what Cole had to tell us. Elliot also wore a concerned look.

"There are rumors that the head of the Yamaguchi-Gumi faction, a Mr. Sam, has quite the interest in rare artifacts focused specifically on Polynesia and Micronesia. He has a special affinity for artifacts steeped in mysticism. According to a report I ran, he recently transferred a large amount of U.S. dollars to a reserve account to take part in an underground art auction held at a private residence on the Mauna Kea resort. He and Wainwright run in similar circles, and both attended the auction. What I'm about to tell you is going to be released to the media tomorrow, but I'm sharing it with you now so you can keep an eye out for anyone suspicious."

He paused, letting it all sink in. My mind spun—what the *fuck* was going on?

"Apparently, this auction advertised a very rare, very powerful, ancient war club owned by King Kamehameha the First, rumored to be imbued with his blood and mana. It's very sought after, and rumor has it, when paired with a rare piece of Hawaiian jewelry, a shark pendant carved by King Kamehameha, the wearer is thought to gain unlimited power."

Shit, shit, shit. This was not good. No wonder Lani wanted to hold on to the Lei o mano and keep it out of anyone else's hands. I wondered if she knew anything about the pendant. And also—would she be able to protect the war club, and herself at the same time?

Elliot's question broke into my thoughts. "So, you have a missing magical war club that some dude was killed with, and a Japanese mobster dude is involved? It's like a Harrison Ford movie!" he said, awe clear on his face.

I groaned and moved to pinch him, but he held up the spatula and waved it at me. I narrowed my eyes—just wait until Detective Daddy left. He was going to be in big trouble then.

"Well, we can't say for certain that someone used the war club to kill him, but that is the assumption."

I slid my eyes over to Elliot, remembering what Lani told us last night. Elliot must've been thinking the same thing. We were in way over our heads here and I didn't know how to help Lani without getting her in trouble or having the artifact taken away.

Shit! Lani! Panic welled up in me. My leg started jiggling of its own accord, and a cold sweat broke out all over my body.

Elliot, sensing my panic, shook his head at me and cut his eyes up to the second floor, reassuring me without words that Lani was safely upstairs.

Unfortunately, Cole caught the whole exchange.

"Listen, this is not a game. This guy is dangerous. If you know where Lani is, you need to convince her to come forward. If he thinks she knows anything, Mr. Sam won't stop until he finds her. At least we could offer her protection until we get this mess sorted out."

My whole body went stiff as I felt the blood drain from my face. Lani's life might be on the line. My first instinct was to rush upstairs and look at Lani with my own eyes.

Elliot, sensing my distress, wrapped his arm around me and steered us over to the front door. Cole had no choice but to follow. I was a terrible liar, and I knew Cole could tell I was hiding something from him from the skeptical look on his face. The quicker we got rid of him and talked some sense into Lani the better.

"Thank you for the information. We will be careful and keep an eye out for anything suspicious. If anything comes up, you'll be the first to know," Elliot chirped, his words oddly formal, the effect ruined by the deranged giggle at the end.

I risked a glance at Elliot and then at Cole. Cole set his jaw and narrowed his eyes at us, nodded once, and then left.

Chapter Twelve
SUMMER

"Phew!" Elliot said, slamming the door and leaning up against it. "That was close. Girl, you need a better poker face. You almost blew it."

"*Me?* You could have at least warned me Detective Daddy was here before I came down. I look like a hobo." I fumed, dismay that Cole saw me at my morning worst washing over me.

From behind me, I heard a snort. Lani stood on the stairs, shaking her head and rolling her eyes at Elliot and me.

I plopped down at the counter and put my head in my hands. It's not like I *needed* a man, but so far, all Cole has seen of me is the hot mess side. There's another side that's pulled together. Somewhere. Shaking my head, I asked Lani, "What's the plan for today? I could call in sick and we can go talk to Auntie Miriam."

Lani made a face and shook her head. "No Auntie Miriam. She would just yell at me for getting tangled up in this. The lecture would last for years. No thank you."

Elliot handed both of us heaping plates of coconut pancakes with Lilikoi syrup, my favorite. Lani shoved a gigantic forkful in her mouth and washed it down with scalding hot coffee before continuing.

"I'm going to clear out of here. Don't get your panties in a twist—I'll text you several times a day and let you know what's going on. I'm using my cousin Jimmie's old phone."

Every instinct told me this was a bad idea, but Lani was the most stubborn person I knew next to my dad, and if she had a plan, she wouldn't deviate from it for anything.

She hugged me tight before I left for work and told me to be careful, slipping a small, deadly looking dagger into my hand.

I stared at it for a few moments before looking at her. Her tone was low, and her eyes grave as she said, "I hope you never have to use it. But I want you to have it just in case. Keep it on you all the time."

I walked out the door, looking back at her cozied up on the couch, remote in hand. She threw me a breezy wave and said she'd be gone before I got back from work.

On my way to work, I noticed a non-descript white Toyota Tacoma following me out of the neighborhood. I took three lefts just to make sure I wasn't imagining things. Nope, still there.

Shrugging my shoulders, I headed to work. *Prepare to be bored.*

Heading down the hill towards the highway, the Toyota kept a car or two between us all the way to Mauna Lani drive. The truck went straight as I took a right and turned into the gated area for the Beach Club.

I couldn't figure out why they were following me or what they hoped to gain—I had two days to get the non-existent pendant to them, so why try to intimidate me? If that's what they were trying to do, they'd made a tactical error; the more someone pushed, the more I dug in out of pure stubbornness. It must be the Taurus side of me.

Another thought came to mind; why did anyone think I had this magical pendant? Cole said it was part of a Hawaiian legend attached to the Lei o mano, but how on Earth would I have come across it?

I thought of Cole off and on; I believed he was trust-worthy, and not just because I'd thought about jumping his bones approximately twenty thousand times. *If only I could get Lani to trust him. Then she would be protected, and I wouldn't have to worry about her getting hurt.*

Cole texted to check in on me around lunchtime. A goofy smile covered my face when I read it.

"Hey, sis, you gotta pass gas or something? Your face looks real funny." Brody said. I narrowed my eyes and kicked his shin before I replied to Cole. I passed the rest of the day alternating between worry for Lani and fantasies about Cole.

Towards the end of my shift, a fit, middle-aged man in dark blue trunks sought me out as I walked the shoreline.

"Ms. Jenkins?" he asked, a cultivated, Eastern European accent coloring his words.

Instantly, my hackles rose. I'm not sure why; there was just something about him that set off alarm bells. *And how did he know my name?*

All the lectures from my dad about situational awareness kicked in and I noted the details in front of me; tall, approximately 6'3", lean but muscular, naturally olive-toned skin tanned perfectly, short, dark salt-and-pepper hair styled just so, and expensive mirrored sunglasses that prevented me from seeing his eyes.

"Can I help you?" I asked, proud my voice sounded steady.

He sidled closer; instinctively I took a step back and then kicked myself for giving up ground. His sideways smirk when he noticed made me want to slug him.

"Well, Summer, I hear you had quite the rescue on Sunday. Pulling a dead body from the ocean must've been dreadful."

Knots formed in my stomach at his words. Who was this guy and why had he sought me out?

Attempting nonchalance, I answered, "Yeah. Not fun, but part of the job. Thank you for your concern." I doubted this guy was concerned, but hopefully he took the hint.

"How brave you were to rescue him. There could've been sharks or who knows what else circling underneath." He gave an elegant shiver that didn't quite seem authentic.

"Uh, right. I was lucky, I guess." I smiled brightly at him and started walking toward the lifeguard tower.

I felt him grip my arm tightly, almost to the point of pain. I looked down at my arm and then at him, ready to swing my rescue tube at him. He released my arm at my pointed look and then put both hands up in surrender.

"Sorry, Summer. Forgive me. I'm fascinated by ocean rescues and have more questions. For instance, did the body look funny to you? Were his clothes still on? Did he have any marks on his body? I've never come across a dead body before, and my imagination just runs wild."

"Hey, Summer! The toilet is plugged again!" Brody yelled to me.

I'd never been happier to hear those words in my life. With one last thorough look at the man, I headed towards the bathrooms, the feel of his eyes on me making my skin crawl.

After finishing the seemingly never-ending task, I gathered up my supplies and risked a quick peek to see if the man lurked nearby. Sure enough, he stood near the lifeguard hut, eyes pointed in my direction. *Was he waiting for me?* I groaned loudly.

"What seems to be the trouble, little lady?" Before me, beer belly protruding over ancient swim trunks busting at the seams, stood a linebacker of a man, easily 6'5" and close to 300 pounds. Various levels of sunburn made a calico pattern across his skin, marking him as a tourist.

Sizing him up, I decided he would do for the diversion I needed. Softening my face and gazing up at him from underneath my eyelashes, I said shyly, "My knight in shining armor. You must have good instincts intuiting when a woman is in distress."

If possible, the man seemed to grow even larger, puffing up his chest and then offered me his arm.

I took it and leaned in. "Do you see that man over by the lifeguard hut with the dark blue trunks on?"

The man next to me nodded. "Well, he won't leave me alone, and I'm just trying to do my job. My backpack and phone are at the lifeguard hut, and I need to grab them so I can go home. I know this a lot to ask of a perfect stranger, but would you be willing to distract him so I can get my stuff?"

A wide grin spread across his face. "No problem. I'll take care of it." The slightest hint of a southern drawl colored his words.

"I'm sorry, I didn't catch your name?" I asked.

"The name's Calvin. Calvin Rickles."

"Calvin, my name is Summer," I said, offering him my hand to shake. His giant mitt swallowed my hand completely as he gently squeezed it in response. "Thank you so much for helping me out. Normally I can handle things myself, but he's kind of weird."

He tipped an imaginary hat my way and I watched as the gentle giant marched down to the lifeguard hut and began waving his arms wildly in front of the man and put an arm around his shoulders, steering him away from the hut. The stranger looked in my direction one last time, and even from where I stood, I felt his anger. My gut clenched; the glare he sent my way promised payback.

Chapter Thirteen
COLE

I TOSSED AND TURNED all night, wracking my brain for a reason the Yakuza believed Summer had the pendant, since, from what she said, she'd never met Wainright before pulling him from the ocean.

She seemed frightened and completely clueless when I asked her about the pendant. Enough that I believed her. And not because parts of me stood and saluted when I got close to her, either. I'd been doing police work long enough to trust my instincts, and my gut said Summer wasn't involved, except accidentally.

Questions raced through my head as I laid in my bed. Was Summer's accident on the bridge connected to the Wainright case? It was hard for my mind not to jump to those conclusions; she didn't strike me as someone who regularly involved herself with sketchy people.

The link to Wainright's murder and Summer's accident pointed at a connection to the Lei o mano and the shark tooth pendant. The magical pendant that supposedly gave a person unlimited power. I snorted at the thought that people believed that. The more I thought about it though, the more I realized that as crazy as the legend was, at least two people had believed in it enough to kill.

Eventually I nodded off, and Summer played a starring role in my dreams, a tiny red string bikini highlighting her "assets." My alarm clock jolted me awake; my body protested being woken up in the middle of such an enticing dream, but I ruthlessly tamped it down and stood under a very cold shower until I felt reasonably awake and under control.

As I headed into work, I made a plan of attack. The first order of business was to put some pressure on the Ichiban corporation and get some answers on why a vehicle registered to their corporation was involved in a hit-and-run accident.

After that, though, I wanted to find out why the chief tried to stop me from investigating the Yamaguchi-Gumi faction.

My internal radar had pinged yesterday when the chief asked for an update; he warned me away from investigating Ichiban or any of their other holdings, which I found suspicious.

"There's nothing there. You're barking up the wrong tree and wasting time with this. Your job is to find out who killed Wainright, not chase your tail and spend time with pretty lifeguards." Chief had continued to belittle my investigation, so I tuned him out until I caught the tail end of his diatribe.

"Besides, you're supposed to find Lanikai Davis and bring her in. Find her, and you've found your killer." With that he slapped me on the shoulder hard enough to leave a welt then turned away. The malicious grin he sent my way let me know he knew exactly what he'd done. Old school bully tactics, 101. *Damn, I really hate that guy.*

The morning was spent researching the Yamaguchi faction as well as their enigmatic leader, known as Mr. Sam. My eyes felt like meatballs by the time my partner yelled across the office to me.

"Peterson, you wanna go get some lunch?"

The last thing I wanted to do was take time away from the investigation, but I figured a break might help me clear my head. Besides, Jonah would be a good sounding board.

Jonah and I talked sports on the way to Kona Brewing. Jonah was rooting for the Detroit Red Wings to take the Stanley Cup this year.

"Shit. They haven't had a contending team since 2009. They haven't even gotten to sniff the air surrounding the cup since 2002, dude." I razzed Jonah. To be honest, I didn't care who won, hockey wasn't my thing. But I liked to give Jonah a hard time because he got so worked up over it.

"Whatever. They're going this year. Their defensive line is solid and their forwards are top-notch. It's going to happen."

I snorted at his hopeful tone. The sun glared over the ocean in front of us as we turned off the highway towards the restaurant.

"Hey, Jonah, did you ever hear anything back about the Lei o mano or shark tooth pendant? It sounds like a fairytale to me."

He was suspiciously silent. "Wait—you don't actually believe in any of that nonsense, do you?"

He shrugged his shoulders. "I don't know, dude. Being on this island does something to you. It's like, there's this energy or something. Something I never felt anywhere else. Does it sound far-fetched? Yeah. But from some of the stories I've heard from locals, I'm not going to dismiss it out of hand."

I was dumbfounded that Jonah felt that way, but I decided to let it go for now and focus on the facts of the case and get his take on the rest of it.

"Hmm. Okay. Well so far, what we've uncovered is that Wainright was disgustingly wealthy and attended a mysterious auction that may or may not have sold artifacts stolen from Hawaiian legacies. At said auction he purchased what is purported to be King Kamehameha the First's ceremonial war club. On top of that, Wainright believed the pendant he wore would give him unlimited power when coupled with the Lei o mano. Also, our prime suspect is a server at Mauna Lani that everyone I interviewed swears had nothing to do with his murder." I needed to talk the case out, afraid I was missing something.

Jonah drummed his fingers on the steering wheel and took a moment before responding. "Yeah, so far that sounds about right. I leaned on my informant to get us information about the auction. Who was in charge and what items they sold, as well as who attended. If I don't hear anything from him this afternoon, I'll track him down by the end of the day."

I nodded, looking at the strip mall parking lot in front of us as Summer's pretty face swam in front of me.

"What I need to find out is how Ichiban and the Yam-aguchi family are involved and why they're targeting Sum-mer."

"Summer, huh? You two are on a first name basis?" Jonah teased, a hint of something in his voice I couldn't put my finger on.

I turned to look at his profile. "What's that supposed to mean? You think I'm blowing the investigation by focusing on her?" I asked, the stiffness in my tone causing Jonah to shift in his seat.

"No, man. You're a solid investigator, and if you think Summer needs protection, then I believe you. It's just been a while since you talked about a girl. I can't even remember the last time you went on a date." Jonah said.

It was my turn to shift uncomfortably; dating hadn't been high on my priority list for a while. My last long-term relationship had ended over two years ago, and since then, I'd only dated sporadically.

My phone rang just then, saving me from having to respond to Jonah.

Unknown Caller popped up on my phone. *Hmmm...*

"Hello?" I heard shuffling noises and a ship horn before a voice, too muffled to tell if it was male or female asked, "Is this Detective Peterson?"

"Yessss—" I said, drawing out the word.

"Wainright's murderers drove a dark green Mercedes G-class with a dent on the rear passenger side bumper. Find them before they hurt anyone else."

"I see. Can I get your name?" I asked, my internal anten-nae picking up a thread of fear in the caller's voice.

"Stop chasing your tail and keep Summer safe," the voice ordered before the line went dead.

My chest tightened when I heard the caller say Summer's name. Fear for her washed over me. Quickly, I filled Jonah in and then texted Summer.

She texted back right away.

"I'm fine. All good here."

I couldn't help the smile that crossed my face at her reply.

Jonah and I discussed who could be behind the phone call I received. I had a pretty good idea who might've made that call, but I didn't mention it to Jonah. If I was right, she was no danger to Summer.

After lunch we decided to break off and work on our own lines of investigation. Jonah dropped me at the station and headed off to strong-arm some information out of his informant while I grabbed my keys and drove to Ichiban Corporation headquarters.

I circled the nondescript, three-story building on the outskirts of Kona near Captain Cook. On my last drive by, I saw Chief Takada standing by his car, a petite, pretty, dark-haired Asian girl wrapped in his arms. As I watched, they kissed passionately before he got in his car and drove away. Luckily, he left through the main exit off La'Aloa Avenue and didn't notice me parked right off of the side street near the rear entrance.

Well, that explains a few things, I thought grimly. No wonder the chief wanted me to back off of Ichiban—he had a mistress working for them.

I waited another twenty minutes to be sure he didn't swing back through before I walked into the main entrance and told the receptionist who I was and why I was there.

She took the card I gave her and disappeared through a door to the side of her desk. A few minutes later, she came back.

"I'm so sorry, sir. No one is available to help you right now. Someone will contact you later," she told me, her English pronunciation almost perfect, with only the slightest hint that she was a native Japanese speaker.

I nodded amicably then told her, "No problem, I'll just wait until someone is available." I sat down on the brown leather couch across from her desk and pulled out my phone, willing to wait as long as it took.

She eyed me balefully before typing into her phone. Soon after, two burly Japanese guys covered in tattoos came out to the waiting room and stared down at me. I offered them my most winning smile, which only seemed to anger them, if their flared nostrils and curled lips were any indication.

"No one is here to talk to you today. You go away now," the taller of the two commanded.

"I'm here in connection with a murder and have questions about a vehicle involved in a hit and run related to that case. I plan on staying here until I get answers." I said pleasantly, not moving an inch.

Both men advanced on me, cracking their knuckles, so I stood up, not willing to go down without a fight, when a short, unassuming Asian man wearing a Brooks Brothers suit walked down the staircase behind us.

"Gentlemen. What seems to be the problem here?" he asked, his voice smooth as butter.

"My name is Cole Peterson with the HPD. I'm here investigating a hit and run that occurred yesterday. The vehicle involved is registered to Ichiban Corporation." I reached into my pocket to pull out my badge and the goons grabbed my arms.

"Whoa, I'm just getting my badge." I told them, holding up my empty hands in front of me. The pressure intensified on either side painfully for a split second before they released me. I pulled my badge out and flashed it at the diminutive man in front of me, a Pat Morita look alike.

He motioned with his hand towards the door, and the thugs bowed respectfully and headed back to whatever pit they crawled out of.

"Now then, Detective Peterson, how can I help you?" the man said congenially. The tone of his words didn't match the intense, penetrating stare he sent my way.

I questioned him about the Escalade involved in Summer's accident.

"The vehicle you mentioned was stolen from our lot two mornings ago. The theft was reported to HPD after your inquiries led us to search for the vehicle. Good luck with your case." With that he turned abruptly to head back up the stairs, effectively shutting down any more questions.

"I didn't catch your name," I called to his departing back.

He spun back to me, a measuring look on his face as he answered. "My name is Sampo Yamaguchi, but most people call me Mr. Sam."

My hand stilled on my notebook at his words; a slight shiver running down my spine. When I glanced back up at the man, he just smiled inscrutably before heading up the stairs.

Shit. This day just kept getting better and better...

Chapter Fourteen
SUMMER

"Hey, sis. Why'd you slip out on me like that?" Brody asked when I picked up his call, his tone worried.

"Sorry, Brody. You know that guy with the European accent hanging out by our hut?" I asked.

"He bother you? If he put hands on you, I'll take care of him next time he comes around." Brody promised. I could picture Brody's face right now. Even though he joked around a lot, he protected anyone he considered ohana.

"He grabbed my arm, but he wasn't getting fresh. He kept asking questions about the Wainright rescue the other day, and he acted really creepy. I had my new friend Calvin go over and distract him so I could get out of there without him seeing me. With all the weird stuff going on I didn't want to take any chances, ya know?"

Brody promised to keep an eye out for me when we worked next and then told me about his latest beach bunny conquest. If I rolled my eyes any harder, they would've fallen out of my head while I listened to his story.

After we hung up, I stopped at KTA for some groceries, crossing my fingers my card went through. As I stood in line, I felt someone bump into me hard.

I turned around and saw a large Asian man covered with tattoos behind me, staring at me menacingly. A chill ran down my spine.

"Cash or card?" the cashier asked, dragging my attention away from the guy behind me.

"What? Oh, uh, card." I swiped my card and booked out of there as fast as I could. Walking up to my car, I noticed a twin to the man that bumped into me standing two cars in front of mine. I'd have to pass him to make it to my car.

I looked around; shoppers pushed carts loaded up with groceries, families with keiki walked through the parking lot—he wouldn't try anything in broad daylight, would he? My heart pounded as I walked by the man, giving him a wide berth. His eyes followed me the whole time, no expression on his face.

I jumped in my car and just before I shifted into drive a tap sounded at my window.

"Gahhh!" I shrieked.

The bag boy stood at my window, holding up the bag of groceries I'd left behind. I thanked him profusely and drove away, watching my mirrors the whole time.

By the time I walked inside the condo, I was a bundle of nerves. Grabbing the bottle of whiskey we kept hidden for emergencies only, I poured myself a healthy amount. Closing my eyes, I took a gulp, letting the velvety texture and smoky flavor seep in.

Boom! My heart started racing again, but when I peeked out the window, my neighbor Stan stood looking under the hood of his old clunker, while his buddy gunned the engine, causing the car to backfire again.

I laid my head against the window for a second, taking a slow, steady breath in. *You need to get ahold of yourself, woman.* I berated myself.

Pulling together a small charcuterie board and an enormous glass of wine to follow the whiskey, I headed out to the lanai, the soft light from the setting sun casting a golden glow, infusing peace into the moment.

Elliot joined me a few minutes later, belting an off-key rendition of Taylor Swift's new song.

"You're almost ready for *American Idol*," I said dryly.

Elliot flicked my arm and then grabbed a handful of crackers and cheese off the board in front of me.

"How was your day? Anyone follow you home and try to run you off the road?" Elliot asked, tongue in cheek.

"Har, har," I responded. "But actually, I had something weird happen today. A couple of weird things." I described the interaction between the dude at the beach and then the man at the grocery store.

"I know nothing *happened,* but it felt menacing." I finished.

Elliot screwed up his face in a thoughtful expression. "I mean, it's nothing you can officially report to anyone, but considering what happened the other day, it might be a good idea to let Cole know about it."

Hmm. "I'll think about it. In other news—how did your day go?"

Elliot regaled me with stories of the fancy schmancy clientele who stayed at the hotel and all of their outrageous demands.

"The big shots who rented out the entire sixth floor decided to rearrange the furniture. I guess a few of the "ladies,"—at this Elliot made air quotes, "wanted to turn the hallway into a runway, complete with furniture for their audience to sit on. By the time housekeeping got up there, ten—count 'em, ten—couches lined the hallway, making it impossible for housekeeping to get through and clean. Then, of course, they called down an hour later and complained their rooms hadn't been cleaned. Oy vey." Elliot threw up his hands.

As I listened to Elliot's story with half an ear, I started compiling a mental list of what had happened since I pulled Wainright's body out of the water.

First, I found out Lani had an argument with Wainright, then followed him back to his house, watched him get beaten to death, then grabbed the Lei o mano. She went on the run after being followed, and then two days later I got run off the road and accused of stealing a pendant off Wainright's body. Today, some weird European guy interrogated me at work, and then a tattooed, potential mobster bumped into me at the store while his near-twin was waiting in the parking lot.

"Elliot," I broke into his montage. He stopped mid-sentence to look at me. "What do you think is really going on? I added it up in my head, and nothing seems to make sense. Rich dead dude bids and wins an ancient artifact at a shady auction, other rich dudes want it enough to kill him, then follow Lani to get it back. I'm just not sure where I fit in. Sure, I found his body, but do they think *I* have the pendant or something? And why would they think that? I can't make sense of it."

While we mulled it over, I heard my phone chime. An unknown number had texted:

"Kawaihae Harbor 10am, Saturday."

Attached was a photo of me in my car at KTA. *Ugh—was that a double chin?*

I started shaking uncontrollably. I dropped my phone, stood up, and looked around to see if anyone was watching me. Our lanai faced the golf course, and while I didn't see anyone out at this hour, that didn't mean someone wasn't hiding out there, watching.

Elliot grabbed my phone and read the text, then stood abruptly as well. He gathered up our dishes and steered me back inside before turning me to face him.

"Sweetie, you need to call Cole. This is serious, and I don't want anything to happen to you." His eyes were suspiciously bright, and his voice trembled.

"You're not crying, are you?" I asked, a note of incredulity in my voice.

"No, you big dummy, I'm not crying!" he answered, before grabbing me in a big bear hug and holding on to me.

"I'm fine, Elliot. Promise," I said, patting him on the back. "Honestly, I'm more pissed off than anything. Who the hell do these people think they are, trying to intimidate me like this? Fuck. Them." I ranted, even if my hands weren't quite steady.

Chapter Fifteen
COLE

*"SUMMER NEEDS YOU, BUT **is being too stubborn to reach out.**"*

The text Elliot sent me ran through my head repeatedly as I raced to their condo. As luck would have it, I had been on my way to Wainright's place, putting me fifteen minutes away, tops. Less, if I broke the speed limit. My speedometer said 62mph—I watched as it rose steadily from there.

I laid on my horn at the car in front of me, then passed on the right to get around them. Lucky for me, the shoulder of the road had been widened years ago to accommodate the Iron Man triathlon held in Kona every year.

My tires screeched as I pulled into Summer's parking lot, and I parked partially on the sidewalk in front of their condo unit. Elliot must've been waiting for me—he waved at me frantically as I threw my car into park and hopped out.

"Where is she? What happened?" I demanded, all of my protective instincts rising.

Pushing through the door and past Elliot my eyes traveled over the whole first floor scanning the area for danger. I heard a creaking noise and looked up to see Summer walking down the stairs towards me.

"Are you okay? What's going on?" I asked, scanning her up and down, looking for injuries. Her face screwed up in confusion.

"What the heck are you talking about?" Her eyebrow raised and she looked at me like she was trying to solve a puzzle, then she glanced at Elliot, understanding dawning before she raised her hand as if to stop my forward momentum.

For a moment I continued staring at her, then turned to look at Elliot with a raised eyebrow.

"Summer, show him the text." Elliot ordered.

At first, she shook her head defiantly at him, arms crossed. Elliot made shooing motions with his hands, eyes narrowed at her and lips pursed. With obvious reluctance she handed me her phone with a long-suffering sigh.

"Detective Daddy checked on me at lunch today, I think he's in love with me," I read aloud.

Summer's face turned bright red before she snatched the phone out of my hand and scrolled with her finger before handing it back. I tilted my head at her, lips quirked in a knowing grin before looking at the screen.

My blood turned cold when I read the message and saw the picture of Summer that she clearly didn't know was being taken. I read it again before handing back the phone and looking into her crystal-blue eyes.

"I'm worried," I said, my voice low as I looked at her gravely.

"Me too," she admitted.

"Why didn't you want to call me?"

"I'm a big girl; I can handle things myself."

I shook my head at her—Lord save me from stubborn women.

Elliot spoke up, "Can we put her in protective custody or something?"

Summer immediately shook her head and backed away.

"Unfortunately, protective custody doesn't work that way. I can ask HPD to patrol out here more often, but that's about it. Is there somewhere you can stay, at least until this is resolved?" I asked Summer.

"I'm not going anywhere." Summer crossed her arms and tilted her head, defiance written all over her face.

Bit by bit, I saw her stance and face soften as Elliot and I stared at her, a united front against her stubbornness.

"Listen, guys. I appreciate that you're trying to keep me safe, but I will not allow those creeps to change the way I live my life. I'll pay even better attention than I already am, and I won't put myself in any situations that could be dangerous, but I'm not leaving."

She stood looking up at me, shining blonde hair curled around her face as little tendrils escaped her bun, red lips begging to be kissed, her cornflower- blue eyes narrowed as she looked at us.

"Detective Daddy, huh?" I said, leaning against the wall and smiling at her in amusement.

"Ugh!" She threw up her hands and stomped off to the kitchen, yanking the refrigerator door open and asking if I wanted a beer. My eyes followed her, then caught on her backside as she bent over to rummage through the refrigerator. Elliot cleared his throat just as Summer turned to look at me, eyebrow lifted as she waited for my answer.

"Uh, yeah, sure," I answered. "I'm officially off the clock, so why not?"

A knock on the door caused my muscles to tense up, and I reached for my sidearm. I kept one hand on my gun as I followed Elliot and watched as he peered through the peephole.

He closed his eyes for a moment and took a deep breath before opening it. "Hi, Karen," he said in a high, unnaturally cheerful voice.

There on the threshold stood a tiny woman, no more than five-feet tall, with graying hair and wearing a saggy muumuu that engulfed her.

"I've told you before, my name isn't Karen," she barked, her face scrunched up in irritation.

"There's a car parked on the sidewalk in front of your door. Move it!" she ordered, before turning around and marching off.

Elliot smirked as he watched her walk away, then looked at me. "That's Hilda, our neighborhood HOA leader and all-around Karen."

I shook my head, my lips quivering as I held in the laughter threatening to erupt. Catching Summer's eye, I saw she, too, was trying to hold in a laugh.

"Why do you always purposely rile her up, Elliot? You know she already hates us because you're gay and I'm a loose woman with questionable morals," Summer scolded, her tone mock serious. At this the laughter bubbled over, and we all let loose.

I headed out to move my car, laughing to myself. Once back inside, I asked Summer, "Can we take a minute to talk about these loose morals of yours?" I lifted both eyebrows at her.

Summer playfully swatted at me and I grinned at her.

"Wanna stay for dinner?" Surprised Elliot was inviting me to dinner, all I could do was nod dumbly at first.

"Sure. Can I help with anything?" I asked.

Summer handed me some carrots and a peeler, and we spent the next twenty minutes making dinner. The compact kitchen gave little room for moving around, and I bumped into Summer several times. Each time, my pulse rose, and my mind wandered back to her text about Detective Daddy. I wanted to explore that more, but now definitely wasn't the time, not with a murderer on the loose and Summer's life in danger.

Dinner turned out to be a blast, Elliot and Summer trying to one up each other with their outrageous stories about the tourists they met on a daily basis. Watching them interact, I could tell how fond they were of each other.

During one of Summer's stories, she mentioned a European tourist who told her she'd be considered unattractive in his country because of her height and weight. She was tall for a girl, probably 5'8" and muscular, but from my angle I couldn't see a thing wrong with her. Elliot ranted about the tourist, and I added, "I'm not sure what crack that guy was smoking, but you've been the star of my dreams every night this week."

They both turned to look at me, mirror images of disbelief on their faces, and I realized what I just said out loud. "Just sayin'," I reiterated, looking at Summer unashamed.

The only discordant moment happened as we were sprawled out in the living room watching *50 First Dates.* "Lani said this is the closest version to real Hawaii." Elliot said out loud.

"I'm so worried about her." Summer shrank down, wrapping her arms around herself, her voice small.

Elliot rubbed her back soothingly. "Our girl will be just fine. She told u—" Elliot broke off and looked up at me guiltily before finishing brightly, "She can take care of herself. Everything will work out, Summer. Promise."

Rather than push it with questions and break the spell, I decided to leave it for now. By the end of the movie, Summer was snuggled on the couch next to me, her head on my shoulder, fast asleep. Rather than move, I stayed as still as possible, enjoying the feeling.

When I felt my eyelids droop, I figured I better wake her and get going. "Summer," I whispered softly.

"Hmmm," she muttered, snuggling even closer. Taking a second to drink in the feeling, I caught a whiff of her scent. Wildflowers and vanilla. Lord have mercy, I wanted to sit there holding her all night. Summoning up all the willpower I possessed, I nudged her gently and called her name again.

She roused slightly and gazed up at me with sleepy eyes. Not quite awake, the soft smile she aimed at me caused my heart to squeeze almost painfully. She shifted a little bit more, her breasts now fully pressed against my side as she curled in to me, before abruptly sitting up, hitting my chin with her head.

"Ow." Summer grabbed her head while I rubbed my jaw. "Sorry I fell asleep on you," she apologized.

"I'm not." I told her as I reached over and cupped her chin. I leaned over and brushed a soft kiss on her forehead. Elliot cleared his throat, and I stepped back and gave Summer a smile full of promise. Gathering my keys and phone, I said my goodbyes.

Before I left, I warned Summer, "Be careful. Watch yourself and don't get caught alone, okay?" She nodded seriously at me. I turned to Elliot. "Keep her safe, man."

Chapter Sixteen
SUMMER

His eyes were full of passion, pupils dilated, muscles taut as he pulled me closer to him on the bed.

"Summer, you're everything I've ever wanted in a woman," he whispered in my ear. He brushed a hand softly down the side of my body, naked underneath his. Suddenly, his hand tightened into a fist and he closed his eyes, looking up as if searching for something.

"I don't know if I can go slow with you sweetheart," he said in a strangled voice, his breathing ragged as his well-built chest heaved up and down.

"Then don't," I told him, moving closer, until there was no space left between our bodies.

His eyes darkened and he leaned down, his mouth running across my nipple, my body arching to meet his mouth as his tongue lick..."

"Summer. Summer. Summer!" My eyes popped opened, and it took a moment for me to figure out where I was. Elliot stood at the side of my bed, shaking me.

"Hmmm....what?" I responded sleepily. Only then did I hear an insistent beeping noise coming from the side of my bed where my phone sat.

"Your alarm's been going off for ten minutes and it's driving me crazy. Get up already!"

I rolled over and shut it off, watching as Elliot gave me one last look from the doorway.

"Hmph!" he ground out before shutting the door behind him.

I laid back on my pillow, trying to recapture the delicious dream. When I found myself cuddled up to Cole last night after I'd fallen asleep, I couldn't help but notice the hard muscles and his scent—pine and ocean and fresh air. Whatever it was, I needed a bottle just to sniff now and then.

I smiled at the easy way he'd fit right in, joking and giving Elliot and I equal amounts of grief, coupled with his obvious sense of duty and responsibility- I'm pretty sure he's why the expression swoon worthy was invented. Which is probably why I spent the whole night dreaming about him. I covered my face with my pillow and groaned.

Cole was a complication—he wanted to find my best friend and interrogate her, and there was no way I'd give up any information about her. Deep down inside, I knew Cole would protect her from whoever the actual killer was, but I also knew his hands were tied as a police officer.

The problem was, although my brain understood this, my body had different ideas. Also, Cole was a good guy. A white knight. When he'd showed up at our house last night, frantic because of the text Elliot sent him, I glimpsed the real guy underneath the badge. He cared. I wasn't just a case to him.

My thoughts strayed to him repeatedly as I got ready for work. I thought about the look on his face when he accidentally read the text I sent to Elliot where I'd called him Detective Daddy.

Based on the way he pulled me in closer on the couch last night, he must feel attracted to me as well. If only he wasn't investigating my best friend...

"Summer! If you don't get down here right now, I'm throwing your breakfast in the trash!" Elliot threatened from downstairs.

"Geez! Hold on! I'll be down in a minute!" I hollered down to him. What had him in such a tizzy this morning?

Hurriedly, I threw on some clothes and headed downstairs. Elliot stood at the counter, flipping pancakes onto a plate. *Thud.* He threw the pan in the sink and slammed the cupboard door closed before turning to look at me.

"Hmph." His gaze traveled up and down before he shook his head slightly and turned back to the sink.

"Dude, what is your problem this morning?" I watched as the water sloshed over the edges of the sink from his vigorous scrubbing, the speed of which increased after my question.

"Problem? What makes you think I have a problem? Just because some of us actually have to keep the household running while others are off having adventures and making new friends doesn't mean I have a problem."

My scrambled brain tried to make sense of his words. What adventures was he talking about? Getting run off the road and stalked by the Yakuza?

"Wait—are you mad because I'm very unwillingly involved in a murder investigation?"

"Of course not. That would be silly. I'm just tired of doing all the work around here while you're off making new friends." Elliot said, his eyes glued to the pot in front of him.

Guilt immediately took over. Was he feeling left out somehow?

I made my way over to him and wrapped my arms around his waist from behind. "You're my best friend. I'm sorry if you feel like I'm leaving you out of things. So much has happened in such a short time that I feel like I'm just ping-ponging through it all."

He stopped his energetic scrubbing and stood still for a moment. He turned and held me in front of him, his soapy hands leaving marks on my T-shirt.

"Your hair looks like a bird's nest, and your morning breath is horrible." He leaned over and kissed my forehead. He handed me a glass of juice and sat down at the counter. My eyes followed his movements, trying to figure out how to make this right.

"Ell—"

"Summ—"

We both smiled and I said, "You go first."

Sipping slowly from the glass he held, his face went through a myriad of expressions before he said, "I'm jealous. Watching Cole be so competent and handle everything, handle *you*, with such finesse, makes me feel like I'm getting left behind, like I'm in the shadows. Usually we do everything together."

"Elliot, you're the only reason Cole even came over yesterday."

Coffee burned my throat as I took a big swallow, hoping the caffeine kicked in fast—I didn't want to say the wrong thing. Elliot may be a bit of a diva, but underneath the glossy veneer he had a heart of gold and always looked out for everyone. Looking at it from his perspective, I could see how he might feel left out.

"From now on, I'm going to do better. You *are* the person I go to for everything. And I promise that I'm not intentionally leaving you out, I'm just flying by the seat of my pants. Your opinion matters most to me, and I'm sorry if I caused you to doubt that."

Elliot's eyes met mine. "I'm worried about you, about Lani. A *murder?* This is so far over our heads. And I really like Cole, and I know we need his help." He fiddled with his napkin, slowly shredding it into pieces, his voice uncertain when he said, "But maybe you don't need me."

Instantly I rushed over to hug him, turning his face towards mine when he refused to meet my eyes. "Of course I need you! You and Lani are my best friends in the entire world. Don't ever doubt it." I kissed his forehead and watched as the doubt left his eyes, replaced with hope.

"Are we okay now?" I asked. He avoided my eyes for a second longer before looking at me and nodding, "Yes, but girl you have got to let me do something with your wardrobe, you look like a lolo hobo. Next day off, we need to go shopping for something that isn't made from cotton."

I laughed and hugged him once more. "Absolutely."

My phone chimed. *Brody.*

"Beach is closed for high surf today. You've got the day off. Don't do anything I wouldn't do!"

Even though I needed the money, having an unexpected day off sounded nice.

"Hey guess wha—"

"You want to pick up a catering shif—"

Elliot and I made faces at each other and laughed. "You go first," I said.

"The catering manager just texted me and said she's desperate for help with a catering gig for those Russians I've been telling you about. She can't get enough people to staff it—no one wants to work with them. It pays a lot of money..." he wheedled.

Curious, I asked how much. My eyes widened when he showed me the text.

"Holy shit. Hell yeah, I'll work it. When?"

"Two nights from now. I'll take care of everything, you just have to show up at three to help get everything set up."

Internally I celebrated; I could get my car fixed now, with money left over...

"Wait, what were you about to tell me?" Elliot asked.

"Oh yeah, my shift got canceled today-they closed the beach due to high surf. Wanna go shopping?" I asked Elliot.

He started to speak, but then paused. "What about the Yakuza? I don't want to take any chances with you getting hurt."

In all the excitement, I hadn't given it a thought. "Hmm, good point. What if we take your car? I'll sneak out back and you can pick me up."

Elliot looked uncertain, but excitement at finally getting his shopping fix in won out. "Deal. But if anything funky happens, we abort mission right away." He gave me a stern look, and I nodded. He rubbed his hands together and said, "it's about time you took your fashion to the next level."

Even though I felt comfortable with myself, Elliot had a point—my wardrobe could use a refresher.

"I'm sure this change of heart has nothing to do with impressing a certain tall, dark, handsome detective..." Elliot stated, tongue in cheek.

He caught the towel I threw at him, laughing at me openly now, then snapped me on the butt with it. "Get dressed girlfriend, we're going shopping!"

Chapter Seventeen

COLE

"Peterson!" I heard my name shouted across the station, and my head whipped around for the source. Chief Takada stood in the doorway of his office, his face red. Apparently, the man didn't believe in subtlety or quiet voices. This was becoming a habit.

"In my office, now!" he bellowed, pointing at the empty chair visible through his office window.

"Somebody's in trouble..." Jonah sang in a high-pitched voice. I smacked him surreptitiously on the back of the head as I walked by, steeling myself for whatever was to come. It was way too early in the day to deal with this BS.

Chief Takada crowded me as I walked through the doorway. *Are we in high school?* I thought idly. I sat in the chair he pointed to, positioning myself so that I could turn on my phone recorder.

He stared at me for several moments, his gaze narrowed. I held his gaze, not in the least bit intimidated by him. He broke eye contact first.

"I thought I told you to stay away from Ichiban Corporation. In fact, I *know* I did. I stood right there in the bullpen and told you it was a dead end." His voice was strained with barely suppressed rage. I watched as the veins in his neck bulged. If his face got any redder, he might explode.

"Sorry about that, Chief, just some loose ends I wanted to tie up. You know how it is—investigating requires so much paperwork, and I wanted to make sure I didn't leave anything out." I said drolly.

He looked slightly mollified by that, his posture relaxing slightly before responding. "They're off limits. Do you understand me?" His tone brooked no argument, and I nodded affably as I stood up.

"Get out and focus on finding Lanikai Davis. If you want to find the killer, then find her." he ground out.

I paused as I stood in the doorway. "Oh, hey, I hope you had a nice lunch yesterday." I looked at him meaningfully, then beat a quick retreat before he could respond. *There. Nothing like stirring the hornet's nest to shake things up.*

The chief was right about one thing though—I needed to find Lani Davis. My gut told me she held at least some of the answers I needed to see the entire picture more clearly. If I was right about the phone call from earlier, then Lani was more than likely closer than anyone realized. *And Summer had probably been in contact with her.* I sighed.

I headed out to my truck after checking in with Jonah. He pinned down his source and they set up a time to meet with the auctioneer. He promised to fill me in afterwards and let me know how it went.

My focus today was finding Lani. I caught Officer Kregness in the parking lot.

"Hey, Kregness, do you have a minute?"

"Sure, boss. What's up?"

"Do you know anything about Ichiban Corporation?" I asked.

He shifted his weight and looked over his shoulder before he lowered his voice. "Just what everyone else does. They're a front for the Yakuza. Not a place I'd dig too deep unless you need to," he cautioned.

"Do you know if the chief has any ties?" I asked, then filled Kregness in on what I'd witnessed yesterday.

He whistled through his teeth before answering. "I'd tread very lightly with this one. Whatever investigating you do you better be as quiet as possible about it." His face crinkled in worry.

Switching gears, I asked him if he knew where I might catch any leads on Lanikai Davis. I watched as his face closed up at the mention of her name. He put his hand on my shoulder and leaned in.

"That girl isn't the murderer. I've known her since she was a baby. Hotheaded, fierce, stubborn as all get out? Absolutely. But she's not a killer." Conviction echoed in his words. "Look, I'll put the word out with the uncles. If she wants to talk, she'll find you. No need go looking—you'll be wasting your time."

I peered into his eyes, stalwart conviction in Lani's innocence reflected out at me. I hung my head in defeat—the

Hawaiian network of friends and family ran deep and strong. If they closed ranks around Lani, I'd never find her. Nodding stiffly at him, I turned to get in my truck.

"Peterson. Start searching for who wanted that Lei o mano most. That's where you'll find the killer."

The words were meant as a peace offering, and I took them as such. Saluting Kregness, I got in my truck and headed out to Kawaihae Harbor. It wouldn't hurt to poke around and ask some questions.

***

Kawaihae Harbor was teaming with boat traffic—charter boats bobbed up and down in the swell, taking tourists out for whale watching, snorkeling, fishing, and scuba diving. Various operators puttered in and out of the harbor, a normal day in high season. Waves rose and fell with increasing frequency and height, and I shook my head—there were going to be some green passengers on those boats soon.

Scanning the harbor, I noticed a sleek Lamborghini 63 dayboat, shining gold hull bright enough to see from space, with the name *Olga's Dream* painted in glittery script on the side parked in front of a marker with Slip #3 on it. Slip 2 was empty.

A passing fisherman, bucket full of Oama, nodded, "Howzit?"

"Hey, man. Can't complain. Do you by any chance know who docks in Slip 2? My friend asked me to meet them here but..." I gestured at the empty spot.

"The harbor's doing work on that spot. It's been empty for a few weeks. It's County, so it won't be fixed until next April if I were to guess—"

"For real. My road's been torn apart for five months." I shook my head. "That sure is a fancy boat," I said, turning towards Slip 3.

"Oh yeah. Some rich Russian dude owns it. Brought it over from Oahu—bunch of goons in and out on it. He brings the ladies here, and let me just say, they have built-in flotation devices." He nudged me with his elbow good-naturedly.

I cracked a smile, but internally the wheels were spinning.

"Thanks, man." I pretended to look around for my non-existent friend. "I guess I'm not going out on the water today." Disappointment laced my words for his benefit.

He clapped me on the shoulder. "You aren't missing much. Swells getting nasty. Supposed to be twelve to fifteen feet by evening." I nodded and waved as he ambled off.

Lost in thought, the creaking of the dayboat drew my attention. Wainright's business and social partners included several wealthy Russians. Was it a coincidence that a wealthy Russian with a boat was docked this close to where Wainright's body was likely dumped? Like I'd told Summer, I didn't believe in coincidences.

Checking to see if any crew were aboard, I made my way closer, noting a few minor scratches in the otherwise pristine fiberglass, I also noticed a piece of cloth caught in the railing. Looking around to make sure no one spotted me, I quickly hopped on and grabbed the cloth, using a receipt

I had in my pocket to grab it so I didn't contaminate any potential evidence with my own DNA.

A throat cleared behind me. The hair on my neck rose and the muscles in my shoulders immediately tensed. *Shit.*

I turned around slowly and found a man of similar height, piercing blue eyes trained on me, head tilted quizzically, a contemptuous smile in place when he asked me, "Can I ask what you are doing on my boat?"

A rough Eastern European accent blended underneath a more polished British accent. My eyes flicked over to the boatloads of tourists coming and going before landing back on him. My mind raced, trying to come up with an excuse. Just then, a black harbor cat meowed two boats down.

"Fluffy! There you are—what a bad kitty you are!" I said, racing over to pick the cat up, ignoring the fact that it was squirming and clawing to get down. With the cat tucked under my arm I walked back over to the man and held up the increasingly angry cat, paws and claws and teeth all engaged in the mission of tearing my shirt to shreds.

"Sorry, man. My cat..." I shook my head. "Well, as you can see, she's quite a character. I feel like I'm always chasing her down."

"It would appear as if she has little fondness for you," he commented, a look of scorn on his face.

Clutching the cat, I maneuvered around him and back to my truck. As soon as I set the cat down in my truck, it howled and attacked the window, trying to get out. Keeping one eye on the cat, I checked to see if the man was watching. I caught his eye as he stood in the same spot, suspicion radiating from him, even from here. I lifted my hand in a wave then threw him a Shaka before I drove away, glancing in my mirror and fending off the attacking cat as it tried to crawl up my arm and scratch my face.

I should just drop the cat off at the north harbor. I shook my head. I couldn't do that. Feral cats ran rampant around here, killing the native birds and infecting monk seal with toxoplasmosis. Gingerly reaching for my phone as I parked at the Minnit Stop, I looked up the Humane Society number.

"I found a cat at the harbor and wanted to bring it in, if that's possible," I told the pleasant-sounding voice on the other end.

"Oh, sorry, sir. We've had a huge outbreak of ringworm, and we aren't accepting any cats right now." she replied.

"Is there any other place that I can take her?" I asked.

"Unfortunately, we are the only cat shelter right now, several others have either closed down permanently or are in quarantine."

I thanked her and hung up, watching as the cat destroyed the upholstery on my passenger seat, her nails raking long tears into it. Saying a silent prayer for patience, I headed for Kona and the pet store.

My mom turned me down flat when I tried to unload the She-Beast on her. "Cole, I'm allergic to cats, and besides, I travel too much to have a pet," she reasoned. "Good luck, though!"

I ran into the pet store, leaving the windows wide open, hoping the cat would be gone by the time I came back. Three hundred dollars later, I peered into my truck, arms overloaded with cat stuff to find it still sitting there, now shredding the carpet on the floors, the fibers pulled up around it, resembling a bird's nest.

I took the cat back to my apartment and carried it in, bribing it into the cat carrier with a cat treat. After making sure it had water I left the apartment to the sounds of a screeching cat. Could this day get any worse?

Chapter Eighteen
SUMMER

ELLIOT HELD UP A tannish-gold silk blouse. "What do you think?"

"It's not your color." My deadpan delivery caused him to roll his eyes and snort.

"Not for me, for you. This color against your tan would be stunning."

Golden shimmery threads sparkled at me. Not my usual style, but I told Elliot I'd try it on. In the dressing room, I quickly changed my clothes. Admiring the shirt, I turned this way and that when something landed on my head.

"Try that on with the shirt," Elliot ordered.

Rolling my eyes, I did what he said. Surveying the completed look, I had to admit Elliot knew fashion and what looked good. My reflection in the tiny dressing room mirror showed a sophisticated woman. The sparkly top was complimented by the white, high-low skirt that hugged me in just the right places. Snagging the price tag from behind me, my heart almost stopped. The skirt cost almost as much as my entire wardrobe.

"Don't look at the price tag," Elliot, mind reader extraordinaire, called from the other side of the door. "Let me see how it looks."

I gulped, but opened the door and walked out, feeling self-conscious. Elliot wolf whistled.

"Now that's what I'm talking about. Am I good or am I good?" he gloated, adding gold bangles to my wrists and then narrowing his eyes, looking me up and down before nodding in satisfaction.

I argued about the cost, but Elliot just whisked the clothes to the register and pulled out his credit card.

"No way, Elliot! I'm not letting you buy that for me."

He smiled. "Just consider me your gay fairy godmother."

The sales associate, a guy about our age with perfectly groomed eyebrows and a better skin care routine than I've ever had, leaned forward. "You definitely have a good eye. Maybe you can help me pick something out sometime." The invitation clear in his tone.

Elliot leaned towards him. "Anytime. I'd love to dress you."

The guy's smile widened, his teeth blindingly white.

The flirting was kind of hot, but I still had a list of things I needed to do.

"Hey, I'm going to just run over to Longs to get some shampoo. Let's meet back up for lunch." Elliot nodded vaguely in my direction, so absorbed by the man in front of him I wasn't sure he was listening. Before leaving the store, I checked the parking lot and surrounding area to make sure no one was waiting to jump out and grab me. The coast was clear, so I headed out.

Venturing out past the chain of stores in the shopping center and taking a shortcut in between Long's and Waimea Coffee, I heard some rustling from the bushes on my left. Wild pigs foraged in this area so I was instantly on guard.

"Summer," a whispered voice called, and Lani's head popped up and then down again, like a whack-a-mole game.

"Meet me behind the building," she ordered from her hiding place.

I looked around casually to make sure I wasn't being followed, then headed at a leisurely pace to the back. I set myself up in a private little area, bushes surrounding a small table and chairs almost completely. Some of the droning on my dad had done when I was growing up seemed to be serving me now. I guess some of it sunk in after all. I could see out, but no one could see in from any distance, the thick foliage from the bushes obscuring their view.

Lani wriggled in to the spot from behind me, crawling through a narrow opening at the bottom. I couldn't help but laugh—this girl was a character. Sobering quickly though, I thought of how much danger she was in.

She swiped dirt off of her clothes before giving me a brief, tight hug.

"You okay, sis?" she asked, worry plain on her face.

"Yeah. You?"

She shrugged her shoulders and quirked her lips in a sardonic smile. "I've been better, I've been worse."

Worry for Lani washed over me and I gripped her hands. "Talk to Cole. He's a good guy and I think he'll listen to your story with an open mind."

Immediately, she shook her head no. "I'm not giving up the Lei o mano, even if it *is* a murder weapon. Besides my fingerprints, I caught my finger on the end of one of the teeth, so now my DNA is on it, too." She paused, her next words surprising me. ""I'm getting off the island. My cousin Sheila and I could pass for twins, and I'm going to use her I.D. to fly to the mainland for a while—disappear until things die down."

"No! I hate that idea. That is the dumbest, most hairbrained idea I've ever heard. Don't go." I wanted to convince her to stay, to talk to Cole and sort everything out. At least if she stayed we could stick together—safety in numbers and all that.

"Sis, there's already heat on Uncle Raymond and the rest of the family, not to mention you. I'm not going to put anyone else at risk. This was my fuck up, and I'll fix it," she said, arms crossed.

She drew in a deep breath and hesitated, and I sensed she didn't want to tell me something. I tilted my head at her in question.

"Auntie Miriam wants to get involved," she burst out, and I sensed her embarrassment.

Despite the seriousness of the situation, I burst out laughing at Lani's expression. Auntie Miriam and Lani were essentially the same person. The only difference being that Auntie Miriam had had time to refine some of her more impulsive behaviors. Most people on the island considered her the highest authority possible.

A beautiful woman in her early sixties, she carried herself with the regal air of a queen, likely not much of a stretch as she was rumored to be a pure-blooded Hawaiian descended from Kamehameha himself. Auntie Miriam was a respected elder in the community, not that she thought of herself as an elder. Her standing in The Nation of Hawaii movement, as well as knowing or being related to most people on the island, meant she had a big sphere of influence. Everyone knew you crossed Auntie Miriam at your own risk.

"It's not funny." Lani pouted.

"It is. It is totally funny. Mom had to get involved." I couldn't help but razz her.

She sniffed and looked away, refusing to meet my eyes. Still looking away she said, "Auntie wants you to meet her at Ichiban Corporation tomorrow at 10:00 am."

My eyebrows winged up in surprise. Shock must've showed on my face as Lani silently laughed at my naivety.

"Summer, you should know by now that nothing happens on this island without her knowing about it. She's going to talk to Mr. Sam and clear things up, island style."

Shit. Island style could mean anything from welcoming you into the family or burning down a building. Auntie was enough of a wild card you never knew which she had in mind.

Reading the myriad of thoughts on my face accurately, Lani grinned. "Yep. Good luck." She patted my shoulder as she smirked.

"But listen, Summer. It's not just Yamaguchi that wants that pendant. Keep an eye on the Russians." And with that cryptic comment, Lani disappeared before I could ask her about the pendant or anything else.

Chapter Nineteen
COLE

"Dude, the guy got spooked. He wouldn't talk. But my informant said he goes to the Blue Dragon every weekend for karaoke and likes to pound 'em back. I say we go there tonight and see if his tongue loosens up after a few drinks," Jonah said.

Dammit. The auction seemed to be the starting point for all of this. I'd hoped Jonah would have more information for me.

Jonah's desk phone rang, and we all stared at it like a museum exhibit. We hadn't used our desk phones in years.

Joah's faced went through several colors as he spoke with the person on the other line. First his jaw fell, then he opened and closed his mouth like a guppy, his face turning from red to ghost white. He hung up and turned to me.

"My gram fell and broke a hip. They have to do emergency surgery, and the rest of my family is off on a cruise. I gotta go." He looked around wildly, picking up a notebook then putting it down, spinning in circles.

"Hey man, let me help. Your gram's in California, right? Let's get you a ticket," I said, keeping my voice calm and steady.

My words must've penetrated. Jonah turned and gazed at me, fear and worry etched on his face. Jonah's gram was his favorite person on Earth. He had a picture of the two of them at Mardi Gras from a year ago on his desk.

"Yeah. Okay. Thanks." He collapsed into his chair, fingers beating out a wild rhythm on his desk.

Once we got the ticket figured out, Jonah shuffled some papers on his desk and then handed me a slip covered in a barely legible scrawl. I looked down at the paper, then back up at Jonah.

"It's the dude from the auction. That's his name and number. You're going to have to fly solo tonight, man. I'm so sorry."

"No worries, I got this," I reassured him.

"Wait—how will I find him at the Blue Dragon?" I asked Jonah as he headed out.

"Can't miss him. Terrible comb-over, thick gold chain, and a gaudy silk Hawaiian shirt opened to his god-damn belly button." Jonah saluted me before disappearing through the door.

Hmmm. The Blue Dragon catered to an eclectic group of people, a little older and wealthier. I would stick out like a sore thumb. An idea sprang to mind, and I grabbed my phone and dialed before I could talk myself out of it.

"Hello?" Summer answered.

"Hey. I know it's last minute, but I need a plus one for a thing tonight."

"Cole? What kind of thing?" she questioned.

I debated whether to tell her my real reason for going, then decided to level with her.

"I got a lead on the auctioneer, and he's supposed to be at the Blue Dragon tonight. He's real skittish, though. I thought maybe if I caught him after a couple of drinks he might be relaxed enough to talk to me."

"And you want me to go with you? Like a date?" she squeaked out.

My palms were slick with sweat. I nodded, then mentally slapped myself before answering. "Yeah. If you're free."

"Uh, sure. I guess so." The uncertainty in her tone made me feel like a twelve-year-old boy asking a girl out for the first time.

"Look, it's not a date date. It's a date in the sense that we'll do something together on a specific day and time, but not like a date with roses and stuff." Even I could hear the defensive tone in my voice.

"Fine. Whatever." By the clipped tone of her voice, I could tell I'd really botched things.

"So, do you think this guy will have any helpful information?" she challenged. "Because if I'm going to get dressed up I want to see some results. My friend Lani is missing," her tone had a weird catch to it I couldn't interpret, "and I'm being targeted for some reason, and now Auntie Miriam is getting involved. Something needs to break loose with this. I just want Lani and my normal life back."

My balls shrank at the mention of Auntie Miriam. A force to be reckoned with, she took no shit from any quarter and would slice through any bullshit in her way. I'd met her once before—she was a stunning woman with an incredible figure, not to mention a seductive air that called men to her like flies to honey. If the rumors were true, men were ruined after one night with her.

If Autie Miriam had involved herself that meant one thing—trouble. *Shit.*

"Cole? Are you still there?" Summer asked.

"Yeah. Sorry. Did you say Auntie Miriam?" My voice may have quivered a bit, but hopefully she couldn't hear it through the phone.

"Yep," she said with obvious relish. *"Auntie Miriam."*

Sweat trickled down my back. Drawing a deep breath, I got control of my racing thoughts to focus on the plan.

"Okay, cool," I said, going for casual nonchalance.

"Mmm hmm," Summer replied.

"So can you go tonight or not?" My voice was gruff.

"Fine. I'll go. Since it's not a date, though, I'm bringing Elliot," she told me.

"Well, my truck only has two seats in it," I told her, crossing my fingers behind my back.

"We can take my car then," she said.

Picturing Summer's clunker, I wasn't sure we'd make it down the block, much less to the Blue Dragon.

"No, we can all squeeze in if I fold up the middle console. It's fine. I'll drive." In fact, this might work out even better. Summer's soft body pressed up against me for the drive? Yeah, this could work in my favor.

Chapter Twenty

COLE

"I'M SITTING IN THE middle," Elliot declared as he maneuvered into my truck. He shot me a knowing smirk when Summer had her back turned.

I nodded stiffly. After all, this wasn't a date, I reminded myself. Most people don't bring their best friends on a first date. Seeing my master plan go up in smoke, I decided to just roll with it and try to enjoy myself, even if I was technically on a case.

"Just keep your hands to yourself." I warned him jokingly.

I looked over at Summer standing next to the passenger door. She had a gold, shimmery top on that warmed her skin and brought out her eyes. The shirt dipped low in the front, just enough to tease a man into distraction, not that it took much with Summer. I put my tongue back in my mouth long enough to say, "You look great, Summer. I like that top on you."

Elliot shot her a triumphant look and she quirked her lips at him while she fussed with her skirt, smoothing imaginary wrinkles out of it by running her hands up and down on the soft-looking material.

"Thanks," she said, her voice soft.

While I drove us to the club, Elliot and Summer bickered.

"I'm paying you back," Summer said, her jaw set and arms crossed.

"No, you're not. I told you; it was a gift. Just accept it like a good girl and be quiet," he responded.

This set Summer off. After a few minutes of listening to them I interrupted and pointed out the setting sun in front of us. Each sunset was different, but my favorite was when the warm pinks colored the sky with fluffy cotton candy clouds.

Summer and Elliot glanced at each other before looking at me sheepishly.

"We're sorry," they both said in unison, looking contrite.

I laughed at their identical expressions, and we filled the rest of the drive with small talk.

The parking lot was jam-packed with cars, some parked on the road and overflowing onto the boatyard next door. Across the street, cement tanks from the shipping yard marred the view of the ocean, but little streaks of pink and orange stretched across the sky behind it, the colors slowly darkening as the moon rose above.

People streamed in, but one man caught my attention. He was wearing a black Hawaiian shirt with bright pink fuchsias that was open almost to his belly button, the gold chain around his neck barely visible from the volcano of chest hair spilling out. His white seersucker pants were about two sizes too small, outlining his package. Several wisps of dyed black hair covered an otherwise empty scalp.

"There's our man." I pointed him out.

Elliot snorted and Summer clapped her hands over her mouth, but not before a loud guffaw could be heard coming from her. Her eyes lit with amusement at the man we all watched. He took slow, mincing steps up to the entrance, but once he reached the hostess, we watched as he puffed up his chest and leaned his elbow on the podium in front of her, nearly missing and falling over before catching himself.

By this time, Elliot was howling with laughter and slapping his knee, tears streaming down his face.

"Oh my God, oh my God, oh my God..." Summer repeated like a mantra.

I laid my head down on the steering well and prayed. This was going to be a long night...

Chapter Twenty One

COLE

"Ready?" I asked Elliot and Summer. By now they were leaning against each other, shoulders shaking, an occasional snort still coming from Elliot.

I smiled over at them, envious. *What I wouldn't give to have friends like this....* The easy comradery and innate connection brought up something that surprised me: envy.

I shook my head and stopped myself from going down that rabbit hole while I jumped out of my truck and waited for Summer and Elliot to join me. I noticed Summer fiddling with her skirt, which drew my gaze to her long, shapely legs, tanned to perfection. I wondered how far up the tan went....

Elliot snapped his fingers in front of my face. *Busted.* He narrowed his gaze at me for a moment before his face spread into a wide grin.

"So, it's like that, is it?" he murmured.

I gestured at her with both hands. "Of course. Just look at her." She bent over to fiddle with her gold-colored sandal, giving us a perfect view of her *assets*. I took a moment longer to appreciate the view before turning to look at Elliot.

"It's not just that, though. There's just something about her. Her sassy mouth, her loyalty to her friends, the way her mind works. I can't get her out of my mind," I admitted.

Elliot regarded me, the depth of his stare betraying how much he cared for her, before nodding resolutely. "Good. She needs someone like you in her life."

Did I just get Elliot's blessing?

Summer was involved in a major murder investigation, and I knew how stupid it was to mix business with pleasure. But still, something pulled me to her.

"Ready?" Summer looked up at Elliot and I, one eyebrow quirked in question.

Elliot and I both held our arms out to her, and after a brief tussle, she ended up sandwiched between us, arms linked. The hostess, a tiny, dark-skinned girl with a purple flowered dress and a warm smile greeted us.

"Reservations?" she asked.

Summer looked at me and my stomach dropped. I hadn't even thought to make a reservation. *Shit.*

Just then, a beefy Hawaiian guy with kakau tattoos and a loose-fitting, light-blue aloha shirt patterned with white hibiscus walked over and stood behind the hostess, a friendly smile on his face.

"Howzit, Summer?" he asked.

"Oh hey, Troy! Howzit?" Summer's eyes lit up and she disentangled herself from Elliot and I to give the man a hug.

He enveloped her in his arms and lifted her off her feet. I did my best to hold my jealousy in check while I watched.

Elliot, silently tracking my reaction, smirked at me.

The man set her down, then looked up at us. "You need a table, yeah?"

We nodded in unison, and his face split into a wide grin before he grabbed Summer's hand and motioned for us to follow him inside.

Gentle ukelele music played softly on the overhead speakers while the band on the small stage near the back tuned their instruments. Troy led us to a small table to the side of the stage towards the middle of the tavern. It offered a perfect view of people streaming in from the entrance. On the other end sat a long bar, flanked by tiki torches and little colorful lanterns hanging above the bar seating, which was filling up quickly.

Troy leaned in close and murmured something in Summer's ear, his eyes catching mine. They lit with mirth as he leaned in and kissed her cheek, my jaw clenched tight as I watched. If possible, he looked even more delighted by my reaction.

"I'll send Hoku over with drinks. Enjoy the music—after the band plays, we gonna do all night karaoke." He released Summer reluctantly and headed over to greet the other patrons.

Summer looked up as I cleared my throat. "What?" she asked. "Do I have something on my face?" I just shook my head and looked away, trying to rein in the unwanted jealousy running through me.

Elliot nudged me as I scanned the crowd. "There he is," Elliot said, his pitch high and excited. He nodded in the direction and held up his hand, waggling his index finger wildly towards where the auctioneer sat, leaning so far forward he almost fell out of his chair. I grabbed his finger and lowered it before anyone could see.

"Dude," I said. "You gotta play things cool. We don't want to spook him, got it?"

Summer snorted at my words. "Yeah, Elliot, *play it cool...*" She punctuated that by using air quotes. He flicked her nose and huffed back into his seat.

I shook my head in amusement at their antics. Our drinks arrived just then and we ordered dinner, passing a pleasant hour talking story and ribbing each other. At one point I realized how easily we all melded together.

So comfortable, in fact, that I didn't realize until Elliot started looking fuzzy that I may have had one too many Mai Tai's.

"Hey, who's that Troy guy?" I asked suddenly, my voice seeming to echo loudly in my head.

Elliot and Summer looked first at each other and then at me, twin looks of confusion on their faces. Summer looked at Elliot and lifted her eyebrow at him. He shrugged a shoulder at her and then looked at me pointedly.

"Don't do that, guys. I hate when you do that," I whined.

Elliot's voice seemed far away when he asked, "Do what, Cole?"

"Have that whole mental telepathy conversation. You guys do it all the time," I grumbled, reaching for my drink.

Summer quickly replaced it with my water glass instead. I wasn't sure but I think she was laughing at me.

"I just want to be part of the team. I can't do the mind thing yet though. Can you teach me?" I asked, hope ringing in my voice. My water glass seemed to have a hard time making it to my mouth for some reason...

Summer patted my hand like a kindly aunt would do, and I smiled at her gratefully.

"You're so pretty. I bet you smell good too," I said.

Elliot snorted and I whipped my head towards him. I wagged my finger. "You can't hog her, you know. You have to share her with me." Somewhere deep down inside, a warning bell was going off, but for some reason my brain and my mouth seemed to be on two different tracks.

Summer's voice came from somewhere that seemed far away. "I coached Troy's daughter for her lifeguard training. He and his wife and *seven* children are ohana. Now, Cole, I have to go to the bathroom. Do you think you'll be okay here with Elliot for a few minutes?"

"No! Don't go. Stay here with me. Sit real close and let me smell your hair." I patted the empty chair next to me. "Don't leave me alone with Elliot. He's mean to me," I whispered. Or I thought I did. From the look on Elliot's two faces, I wasn't sure.

"I think you'll be okay for a few minutes. Elliot promises to be nice, don't you, Elliot?" Summer said soothingly.

"Fine." I pouted.

As she walked away, I watched her, leaning back in my chair. Just before I tumbled completely over trying to keep her in view Elliot caught my chair and righted it. My head bounced back and forth, and I felt like I was on a boat in rough waters.

Elliot laughed, a smirk on his face.

"She's so pretty. Do you think I have a shot with her?" I asked, closing one eye so I knew which Elliot I was talking to.

"I think you're a teensy bit drunk and you're going to have a lot of regret tomorrow for many reasons." Elliot's prim tone had me shrinking in my seat. Taking mercy on me, he continued. "But I think if you treat Summer with respect, and understand she's scary smart, fiercely loyal, and show her you trust her, then yeah, you might have a shot with her. But definitely not tonight."

"Thanks, man. You're the best. I hope I can have mental telepathy conversations with her like you do," I said. Judging by Elliot's confused face, I'm not sure if everything I said made sense.

Elliot's attention shifted somewhere to my right, and I followed his gaze. Summer sat in the seat next to the auctioneer, twirling her hair while he leered down her shirt. *Shit.* I moved to stand up, but Elliot grabbed my arm and shook his head.

"Let her be. She knows what she's doing. Believe me, if there's any information to get from him, she'll get it."

Chapter Twenty Two

SUMMER

"So, THERE I WAS, sitting between the Crown Prince of Uzbekistan and the head of the Inagawa faction, playing them off each other. I pulled in three million just on commission alone for that one," the man bragged, swirling his drink and leering down my top.

"Oh wow, Albert. You're so smart!" I giggled as I twirled my hair.

I pretended to sip the drink in front of me and then leaned forward. "I heard that dead guy they pulled out of the water the other day was rich, too." I sighed for effect. "I bet it's so nice to have enough money to buy whatever you want, to feel so free." I leaned even closer. "I love to feel free. Sometimes, I feel so free I go skinny dipping in the ocean," I whispered near his ear.

He bobbled his drink a little and puffed out his chest. "That guy had money, but no sense. He thought the artifacts he bought were going to bring him some sort of magical power." He snorted. "All it brought him was death." He held up his glass to the bartender and jiggled it. "But me, I know better. It's just merchandise to move. Sell it to the highest bidder and make sure you drive up the cost as much as possible." He eyed me up and down. "Now a girl like you, with refined taste, you deserve a man like me. A man that doesn't live in the make believe world."

I batted my lashes at him and angled away from him an inch. He tried to lean towards me but almost fell off of the barstool.

"Well, my cousin told me there were a bunch of high rollers at some auction on the island. I bet it was that one. The dead guy probably didn't have much competition—I mean, it's just some dumb old stuff someone probably found in their attic or something."

"Ha! Quite the opposite. I thought for sure guns were going to get drawn. Wainright's lucky he got out alive, between the Russian guy and his thugs and Mr. Sam. They all wanted that Lei o mano. I still don't know how Wainright had enough capital to win the bid." He shook his head, perplexed.

A look crossed his face after he finished talking, and he glanced around wildly. He seemed ready to bolt so I put my hand on his thigh and stared into his bloodshot eyes as if he were the most fascinating man in the room.

"Oh, Albert. I don't think anyone appreciates how smart you are," I said, running my fingers up and down his leg. He took a big swig of his drink and immediately started coughing and choking. I leaned back to avoid the splash zone.

Once he got himself under control, he straightened his shirt, looking hopeful when he asked for my phone number. I scribbled Jessica's name and phone number on a napkin and handed it to him. Okay, so maybe I wasn't fully done with my revenge.

He held it up to the light, closing one eye as his hand swung wildly. "Better put this somewhere safe," he said, hand heading for the front of his pants.

Just as I was ready to hop up and call it a night, because let's face it, no one needed to see that, he pulled a small pouch out of his front pocket and placed it inside, almost reverently.

He caught my glance and patted the pouch gently. "All of my treasures go here," he told me.

Just then, Troy came on stage and announced they were starting karaoke. Albert started bouncing in his seat, his face lit up with excitement.

"To start us off, we have our number one fan favorite, Albert Moore!" Troy proclaimed, his arm sweeping across the room to point right at Albert.

People clapped politely, and Albert hopped off his stool to head to the stage. He turned back after a few steps. "Stay and watch me?" he asked shyly.

I nodded, feeling a little guilty.

Albert was in his element, he sang song after song, and the crowd loved him. He really got into it—strutting across the stage and shimmying. His singing voice wasn't terrible, and I had to admit he was kind of fun to watch.

Elliot waved wildly at me, and I saw Cole grinning my way, giving me a thumbs up. *Oh boy.* I got the information

I'd wanted, and if we didn't leave soon, Cole would need to be carried out to his truck.

While Albert was distracted by his fans, I weaved my way through the crowd and told the boys it was time to go. Elliot stood up, holding out a hand to Cole. Cole scoffed, then knocked his chair over getting up. I rolled my eyes at him, and he just continued to grin stupidly at me.

"Come on. You can do it," I told him as I led them both out the back door and to the truck. There was a brief struggle to get Cole to hand over his keys, but once Elliot and I got Cole stuffed inside, he fell silent, staring at me as I drove.

"What?" I asked, irritated.

"I like the way you handle my truck," he said, his voice suggestive. Elliot smacked him on the back of the head and Cole quieted.

Two blocks from home I noticed Cole was looking a little green.

"You okay?"

He shook his head, crazy-eyed. I stopped the truck just in time for him to hop out and throw up most of dinner and possibly lunch too. We waited until he finished retching, his face pale and embarrassed.

Once we got home, Elliot and I pulled the couch bed out and made it up for Cole, handing him a bowl and putting a glass of water and some aspirin on the end table near his head.

He hung his head, eyes downcast and a little sad as he looked at me when I told him goodnight.

"Sorry, Summer," he said, his voice small.

I leaned over and kissed his forehead. "Happens to all of us, believe me. But tomorrow I am going to tease you mercilessly."

He nodded and snuggled into the bed, soft snores coming from him almost immediately after his head hit the pillow.

Just before I fell asleep, my phone chimed.

"Made it to the mainland. See you in a few months."

Chapter Twenty Three
COLE

THE SMELL OF BACON frying woke me up. I laid still, trying to figure out where I was. Little snippets of last night came to me, and I groaned. The noise bounced around in my head like a bowling ball.

Cracking one eye open, I noticed a glass of water and aspirin on the end table and grabbed both, gratitude filling me.

"How you feeling this morning, big guy?" Elliot asked, worlds of snark in his question.

"Like I got run over by a truck and dragged behind it," I told him.

Elliot laughed and I shushed him, the noise causing pinpricks of pain in my brain.

I thought about last night and realized I'd blown my chance to get any information from the auctioneer. And Summer probably hated me. A fuzzy memory of her kissing my head came to mind, and I hoped maybe she wasn't too mad at me.

With my head cradled in my hands, I sat up slowly, making sure not to jiggle my head too hard. A running list of all the ways I screwed up ran through my head.

"Dude, what the hell was in those Mai Tais? I'm not saying I'm a heavyweight, but I can usually handle my alcohol better than that."

Elliot flipped four pancakes onto a plate, then added some slices of bacon and pushed it in my direction.

"Ahh, see you don't know Troy like we do. Did you happen to notice that we stuck to one cocktail and then switched it up to sparkling water? Troy serves his homemade rum, uses the sugarcane from his Ohana legacy farm in the Mai Tais. He distills it until there aren't any impurities. The alcohol content is something like 160 proof, but it's so smooth it sneaks up on you. Everyone knows that."

"Jesus, I think I'm dying," I moaned.

Summer's laugh floated down the stairs and when I looked up at her, I swear there was a halo around her head. Sunlight streamed in behind her and I squinted against the light, a hand on my forehead to shade my eyes.

Lord, she was beautiful, hair swinging long and wavy over her shoulders, tanned skin highlighted by eyes so blue I swear I was looking into a glacial lake. My heart pounded. *God, I hope I didn't blow it with her.*

"Hey there, how's our little lush today?" Summer teased, ruffling my hair as she walked past me to the kitchen.

"If I buy you a new car, can we never talk about this again?" I begged.

"You wish, lightweight. I plan on giving you shit about this for a looong time." She replied.

A brief glimmer of hope sparked. Did that mean she wanted me around for a long time?

A beep sounded from the pale-yellow leather purse Summer was carrying. Quickly checking her phone, she groaned and grabbed a handful of bacon as she headed for the door.

"Wait," I called after her, just then noticing the flowy skirt and soft pink top she was wearing. "Where are you going?" I asked, my tone demanding. Realizing how that sounded, I tried again.

"What I meant to say was, with the Yamaguchi-Gumi and who knows else tracking you, I'm concerned about where you're going because I don't want anything to happen to you."

"Awww." Elliot clapped and wiped a fake tear from his cheek. "She's already got you wrapped around her little finger."

"Shut it. I'm worried about her safety, that's all." My eye started to twitch.

Summer came back over and gave my cheek a little pinch. "That's so thoughtful, big guy. But don't worry, I'll be with Auntie Miriam."

A look of horror must have crossed my face, because Summer and Elliot both laughed hysterically at me.

"What?" I said defensively. "She's scary!"

Summer gave a cheeky little wave and flounced out the door, leaving me alone with Elliot. With some trepidation, I looked his way.

"I'm willing to share her with the right guy," he said. "But if you mess up and hurt her, I will set all the Miriam's on the island on you," he threatened. I froze. *Could he really do that?*

I shook my head, trying to clear some of the fuzzy little cobwebs out of it before replying. "Deal. Because that's not the type of guy I am. If I was, I wouldn't even think about going after a girl like Summer," I reassured him.

Elliot just nodded and gestured at my nearly empty plate. I hadn't even realized I'd eaten. "More?" I shook my head then offered to clean up the kitchen and set the couch bed back to rights.

At first, I thought Elliot might refuse, he was silent for a moment too long. "Uh, sure. Yeah, okay. That would be great."

We cleaned in companionable silence, developing an efficient rhythm of washing and drying. After getting the couch sorted, I told Elliot I was heading out.

"What are your plans for the day?" he asked.

"Shit, shit, shit!" I swore, remembering I had a cat in my apartment.

"That bad?" he asked, amused.

"I just remembered I took a cat home from the harbor yesterday and it's locked in my apartment right now, probably tearing everything apart and yowling so loud I'll get evicted." I slapped my forehead. Man, that was dumb.

Elliot recoiled in horror. "A cat? Are you crazy?" He tsked. "You can't leave a cat alone all night—that's irresponsible!"

"I know, I know. It was a thing that kind of got out of control." I replied. "All the shelters were closed because of a ringworm outbreak, and my mom can't take it because she's allergic. It just sort of happened."

"Well, good luck with that." He made a shooing motion with his hands, and I felt his judgement reach across the room.

"Text me if you get any updates from Summer. I'm going to head into the office and see if I can find any of Jonah's notes and get some more details about who might've been at the auction."

Elliot nodded. "Hey do yo—" He hesitated. "I'm making dinner tonight, and I always make too much. If you'd like to join us, you're welcome to come." Even though his words sounded gruff, his face held a hit of vulnerability.

"Sure, I 'd love to. I eat out a lot, so I never turn down a home cooked meal." I told him.

"Dinner's at seven. Don't be late, and, Cole, may I suggest showering before you come over?" he pinched his nose with one hand and fanned the air in front of me with the other, a look of amusement on his face.

"Yeah, yeah," I grumbled.

Once I got into my truck, I checked my phone. I had increasingly frantic texts from Jonah. Apparently, no one in the office realized he'd left and he'd been getting messages all morning about Albert, the auctioneer.

The most recent text was a photo of Albert laying in a hospital bed, face and what I could see of his arms covered in bruises. *Shit.*

Running through the McDonald's drive-thru in Waimea, I grabbed a Coke and some fries, my personal hangover cure, before heading to Queen's hospital. The admitting clerk called the nurse to let them know that an HPD detective was there for Albert.

While I waited, I walked in circles around the lobby.

A woman in her late fifties, with tired eyes and a no-nonsense look on her face approached.

"You can come on back, but don't stay long. He's in awful shape and I'm not sure how much energy he has to be interviewed."

I nodded. "Of course. I'll do my best to be as quick as possible," I reassured her.

She stopped in front of a patient doorway suddenly. "I hope you catch whoever did this. Albert comes across as a blowhard, but he can be really sweet. We try to watch him sing karaoke as often as possible. My auntie has a huge crush on him."

When I stepped into his room, I tried not to let the shock show on my face. Albert had all kinds of tubes and hoses sticking out from him. As I moved closer to the bed, he cracked open his eyes slightly, a look of recognition passing across his face.

"I saw you at the Blue Dragon last night," he said.

"Yep, I was there with my friends," I said. "I think I heard you sing, but my memory is a little fuzzy."

"Ahh, Troy's rum got the better of you," he said knowingly, his eyes lighting up with mirth.

"Sure did. Wish someone would've warned me," I told him good-naturedly.

He laughed, which quickly turned into a coughing fit, the machine above his head beeping loudly as his face got red.

The nurse came rushing in and glared at me before getting him settled. "Five minutes," she commanded before leaving the room.

I stood at Albert's bedside and surveyed his injuries. Bruises covered him from head to toe from what I could see. I whistled. "Someone sure did a number on you. Can you tell me what happened?"

He nodded carefully before answering. "I finished singing and went back to the bar for my jacket. I noticed a tall guy dressed completely in black watching me, but didn't pay much attention. The aunties were crowded around, asking me to sing one more, but I needed to get home to feed my pet pig, Penelope. If I don't feed her precisely on time, she gets into things. I don't know how she does it, but she somehow manages to escape her enclosure. I rushed out to my car, worried about my new curtains. She loves curtains. Third time I've replaced them in a year." He motioned towards a glass next his bed and I held it for him and watched while he took a small sip through a straw.

"So anyway, just as I reached my car, the big guy from inside grabbed me and accused me of 'telling tales out of school', or something like that. I couldn't understand exactly, he had a pretty thick accent. I don't remember a whole lot after that. I guess some aunties saw what was happening and rushed out before he could kill me."

"Do you know approximately what time this happened?" I asked.

"It was just after midnight. Penelope gets fed every six hours and I was running late."

"You mentioned the man had an accent—can you describe it for me?"

"He sounded Russian, and his English sounded almost exaggerated, like he learned English in the U.K."

My gaze sharpened. "Can you describe him?"

"Like I said, tall, crew cut, but I couldn't tell you what color his hair was, and he had dark, cold, mean eyes." He paused for a moment. "Oh, and he had a tattoo on his hand, a scythe, I think."

The nurse poked her head in. "Time's up." I nodded and said my goodbyes to Albert and promised to follow up with him about anything I learned.

As I turned to go, Albert asked tentatively, "Do you think Penelope will be okay? My neighbor said she'd look in on her, but I'm worried how she'll do alone."

I offered to check in and Albert said he'd text his neighbor to let me in and we said our goodbyes.

Walking to my truck I thought about what Albert told me. The puzzle pieces, instead of coming together, were just getting weirder and more oddly shaped.

Chapter Twenty Four

SUMMER

Auntie Miriam stood in the Ichiban Corporation parking lot next to her bright red late model Cadillac Luxury CT4, tapping her foot and looking at her watch. Glancing down at the clock in my car, I gulped and then made eye contact with Auntie Miriam. Big mistake. She turned the full power of her stink eye at me, and as soon as I stepped out of my car, she unloaded.

"Why you no here on time, eh, Summer?" she scolded.

"Auntie, it's 9:59. You said 10:00. I'm actually a minute early," I finished brightly.

"Bah!" She shook her finger at me. Auntie Miriam tolerated exactly no bullshit from anyone. And even though I was technically on time, in her mind, if you weren't there fifteen minutes early you were late.

She rummaged through her purse and then grabbed a plumeria print chiffon scarf and handed it to me.

I looked at the scarf in my hand and then back to her. "What do I do with this?"

Instead of answering she mumbled something unintelligible that sounded suspiciously like "useless child" and then tied the scarf in some intricate knot around my neck that I'd never be able to recreate. Turning to look at myself in the car window I had to admit that it added some extra quality that finished the outfit in a way that screamed elegant sophistication in a way I never could.

She snagged my arm and steered me towards the main entrance. "Now let me do all the talking. Got it?"

I nodded, still confused and impressed that she could make a simple scarf turn a basic outfit into something special. She noticed me fingering the scarf and said, "Take it from me, you won't always have youth and smooth skin. A sense of style stays with you forever."

The door chimed as we entered, and a pretty Asian receptionist greeted us.

"Can I help you?" she asked, her Japanese accent barely discernable underneath her posh British accent.

Auntie Miriam smiled charmingly and said, "Yes. We have an appointment with Mr. Sam at 10:00."

The receptionist lifted her phone to make a call when an older Japanese man, wearing a well-fitted dark gray suit and bearing an uncanny resemblance to Pat Morita, came into view. (For those of you who don't know who Pat Morita is—he's an iconic Japanese American actor who played Mr. Miyagi in the classic *Karate Kid movie.* Lani's dad played it on repeat-it was the only thing he let us watch when he was around!)

"No need to call, Naomi." The man bowed slightly in front of us and then held out his hand to Miriam. She took it delicately and the man gazed first down to where their hands were clasped together, and then up to her face, mesmerized.

She smiled almost shyly at the man, and I did a double take. Since when was Auntie Miriam shy around anyone?

I cleared my throat and they both startled, his bushy gray eyebrows lifting in alarm or embarrassment before gently letting go of Miriam.

"Noriyuki Ueki?" Miriam asked.

"No, my name is Sampo Yamaguchi, but you may call me Sam," he said shyly.

"Sampo, Sam. Thank you. I was referring to your suit. Is that a Noriyuki Ueki design?"

He looked down at his suit as if just realizing he was wearing one before his eyes darted back to Miriam's. "Yes, it is. You recognize his work?"

She reached over and fingered the sleeve and button on his right arm delicately. "Yes, fine workmanship. His work is incomparable."

My eyes tracked between the two. At this point I felt like I was watching some sort of secret mating ritual and was equal parts entranced and uncomfortable. Auntie Miriam continued to examine the stitching and embellishments for several more moments until I cleared my throat and she stilled, then slowly and languorously trailed her finger down the material and back to her side.

"This young lady is Summer Jenkins," she introduced me. Mr. Sam bowed again and offered his hand. His firm grip was impressive for a man his age, but the shake lasted only a moment before his eyes strayed back to Miriam.

"Let's go into my office and talk, shall we?" He ushered us up an elegant, chrome and Koa wood staircase and into a spacious office filled with teakwood furniture and tasteful Hawaiian art.

He gestured to the two seats in front of the massive teak desk. Neatly organized piles of paperwork were sitting on the surface, and a small, framed photo of a younger Mr. Sam and a woman about his age in the photo.

"Can I offer any refreshments?" he asked.

We both shook our head no and he sat behind the desk in an artfully designed chair embellished with chrome and wood accents, matching the stairs we'd just climbed.

He spread his hands wide, an open, friendly smile on his face. "Ladies. What can I do for you today?"

Miriam ran her hand slowly down the side of her cheek, pausing at her neck for a moment before running her fingers softly through her hair, then turned the full power of her gaze on to Mr. Sam. He looked frozen in place, and I did my best not to smirk as I watched this obvious display of Auntie's feminine power.

"My friend Summer, whom I consider *family*," emphasizing the word family, "believes that someone within your organization may be targeting her and trying to harm her or my niece Lani. Is that true?" she asked, looking directly at Mr. Sam, her gaze piercing.

"My dear, Ms. Hanalei..." Sam began.

Miriam interrupted. "Please, call me Miriam," she said, her voice throaty, seductive.

Mr. Sam straightened in his seat and continued. "I believe there has been a big misunderstanding. I was initially given information that Ms. Jenkins and your niece may have some items belonging to me. Further investigation has revealed that is unlikely to be the case. My apologies for any inconvenience or upset this may have caused you, Ms. Jenkins." He bowed from his chair. "I consider this matter closed, and as a further show of goodwill, I would like to place both ladies under my protection."

Whoa. What? Protection from someone in the Yakuza? I'm pretty sure there's a handbook on life somewhere that says to stay far away from Japanese mob bosses and if they offer you anything—run.

"What exactly does that mean?" Visions of big goons following me everywhere played in my head.

My leg started bouncing of its own accord. Auntie Miriam reached over and placed a hand on my knee, stilling the movement.

"Ms. Jenkins, my men will be available to you if you have need of protection at any time. They will come, day or night to your aid should you be in need of their services."

I sat back in my seat. Okay, that didn't sound so bad. I'd probably never take him up on his offer, but at least he didn't want to run me off the road anymore.

"Thank you," I said, and then, because I guess I like to push my luck, I asked, "Do you know who might be involved in Wainright's murder?"

Miriam immediately smacked my arm, and Mr. Sam's face closed down, a bland expression replacing the previous open smile.

"That, my dear, is none of my business. And none of yours, either. May I offer you a piece of advice?"

Whatever he had to say I had a feeling I wasn't going to like, but I nodded anyway.

"Whomever killed Mr. Wainright is powerful, with many resources at his disposal. You would be wise to keep your nose out of this." The earlier charm had disappeared, and in its place I could see the version of Mr. Sam that men feared. The glacial look in his eyes warned me away from asking any further questions.

He stood up, a silent announcement that our meeting was over. He opened the door and escorted us back down the stairs, lingering as he said goodbye to Auntie Miriam. I drifted towards a glass case that held an intricate metal helmet, a placard in front stating it was a Kawari Kabuto helmet from the Edo period in the 17th century.

While I examined the intricate designs etched on it, I heard Miriam purr and then giggle. *Giggle.* I looked around to make sure I wasn't in some alternate universe.

Mr. Sam and Miriam came to stand next to me. "That is a family heirloom, as you call it here in the United States. My many greats grandfather wore it to fight in the Boshin War."

We all gazed at it for a moment and then Miriam commented, "What a beautiful piece."

"I have more." Mr. Sam's voice held a bashful note and his eyes looked hopeful as he said, "I'm happy to show you my collection any time, Miriam."

A snort escaped me, and Miriam pinched the inside of my arm as Mr. Sam turned away, looking slightly embarrassed.

"I would love that," Miriam said softly, placing a hand gently on Mr. Sam's arm. His smile stretched wide as he bowed to her, taking her hand and kissing the back of it like in some old-fashioned movie. It was kind of cringy and sweet at the same time.

We took our leave, walking to the parking lot slowly. Mostly because Miriam kept turning around to see Mr. Sam. Every time she looked, he was watching her, his eyes following her progress with an inscrutable look on his face.

I reached my car and opened up my door to get in when I heard my name being called and Mr. Sam came running out, any sense of dignity lost in the mad dash to reach us.

"I forgot," he said. "Hand me your phone." He held out his hand to me. I recoiled, not wanting to, but gave in under the harsh glare of Miriam's glare. He tapped a few things on the screen and then handed it back.

"I programmed in my phone number and an emergency button that will ping your location to my men."

He tentatively held out his hand to Miriam, gesturing towards her phone. Without hesitation, she handed it to him, a gesture of faith that he recognized, bowing slightly with a pleased look on his face. When he finished, he handed the phone back to Miriam, his hand lingering on hers for a moment before he waved us off.

As I drove out of the parking lot, my phone dinged. *Lani.*

Hope Auntie didn't steamroll you too bad. Better you than me!

Chapter Twenty Five

COLE

THE STATION WAS PRETTY quiet when I arrived, balancing a giant cup of coffee and the cat carrier containing one furious cat, if the yowling, screeching, and general hissing were any indication.

"Yo, Cole, I didn't know it was bring your girlfriend to work day!" one of the other officers said, smirking.

I flipped him the bird and set the carrier down next to my desk before taking a giant gulp of coffee, the scalding hot liquid burning my throat. I glanced around, relieved the chief wasn't around. I didn't have the bandwidth for that dude right now.

Clank. The cat carrier flipped on its side as the cat fought to escape his kitty prison. When I'd walked into my apartment earlier, the cat had somehow broken out of its crate and I found him laying on my couch, fully spread out, licking itself like some cat porn movie. The damage was extensive. My curtains were shredded, my favorite recliner scratched, things overturned, and somehow the water in my kitchen sink was running, dangerously close to over-flowing. My only option was to bring her in to work with me and hope I could find some sucker to take her off my hands.

"I don't know if she likes you much though, buddy. Might think about getting a new lady," Kregness teased.

"You know anyone who wants a pet cat?" I asked him. "She's real friendly," I lied as the volume of her hissing increased.

Kregness chortled before answering. "Yeah, no, I think I got enough ladies in my life with attitude. Don't need to add any more."

"What about you, Thompson? Don't you have a little girl? I bet she'd love to have a little kitty," I asked desperately.

"No can do, buddy. My wife would cut my balls off if I brought home a cat," he answered.

Dammit.

"Hey. Any of you catch the case of the guy that got beat up over in Kawaihae last night?" I asked the room at large.

Thompson raised his hand. "Yeah, that one was rough. Poor guy. My auntie loves that dude."

What was it with Albert and women of a certain age? I shook my head.

"Do you mind if I look at your notes? I think his beating is connected with the Wainright murder."

"No man, go ahead." He handed over some papers and then copied a flash drive and handed it to me. "This is everything I have so far. Let me know if you find anything."

I nodded at him, then grabbed my laptop, backpack and the damn cat and headed out to the truck.

Bright sun poured in, heating the cab quickly. I rolled down the windows and headed towards Albert's place, a wealthy little subdivision in Waimea. I keyed in the gate code Albert had texted me and made my way toward a single-story, plantation-style home, painted dark green with white trim. The house lay centered in a spacious fenced lot and surrounded by citrus trees and lilikoi vines climbing the corners of the fence.

As I pulled up, an older lady, gray ponytail pulled through a golf visor wearing a pink golf skirt and matching polo top ran over from the house next door.

"Oh, I'm glad I caught you. I'm Barbie. You must be the detective. Here's the keys. Albert said you'd take care of Penelope. Phew. I'm late for my tee time. Take care!" With that she shoved a set of keys at me and spun away quickly before I could get a word in.

I looked at the keys in my hand and then down at the screeching companion in the seat next to me. Setting my shoulders, I lifted the carrier and set it in the shade of the front lanai before carefully unlocking the door and entering the house.

Inside the house, the ceilings soared, making the space look even larger than it appeared from outside. Bamboo and Sapelle wood accents throughout gave the house an authentic feel, the Dickey roof style keeping the house cool.

Snorting, interspersed intermittently with a squeal came from somewhere near the kitchen. I followed the noise to a little room off the kitchen, tile floors leading to a partially enclosed space, with an automatic dog door on the outer wall large enough for the miniature pink pig sitting at the center to fit through. She lifted herself delicately onto her hind legs and wagged her little tail at me, reminding me of a dog.

I reached down to pet her, and she nuzzled against my hand, snorting and squealing happily. Picking her up, I walked over to a food bin and replenished her food and water and watched while she devoured her meal. Leaving her to it, I wandered the rest of the house, checking to make sure the windows and doors were locked.

The house had four bedrooms; one converted into a state-of-the-art office that looked like it belonged in some high rise in New York City. I wandered in, looking around at the built-in bookcases full of books, most veering towards art and history. There were some books on Shibari, complete with photos. Hmm. Albert was an interesting man.

The desk, a monstrosity taking up center stage in the room, sported different colored wood inlays forming a wave pattern on the front, had neat piles of paper on top, and I shamelessly rifled through them, searching for anything that mentioned the auction or attendees.

Underneath one pile, I found a single sheet of paper with a list of items, one being the Lei o mano, and several emails at the bottom.

Ten, to be exact, one of them the same email we had on file for Wainright. Hurriedly, I took a screenshot of them and put the paper back underneath the pile I'd found it in.

Snort, snort. I looked up from the desk to see Penelope standing at the entry, her little tail spinning wildly.

"How did you get out of your pen, you little sneak?" I asked her, mystified.

She snorted again and then came over to rub herself on my legs. I moved to her pen in the kitchen, and she followed me until suddenly veering off towards the front door, where the cat could be heard yowling and screeching. Penelope looked up at me with rounded eyes, and seemed to whimper, if that was even possible.

"No way." I shook my head. "That she-beast will tear apart this whole house," I told Penelope.

Snort, snort. I looked out the window next to the door, only to see the now crate-free cat clawing frantically at the front door. I flung it open to grab her and get her back in her crate, but she darted nimbly past me and ran straight to Penelope. My heart was in my throat as I chased after her, hoping to God the She-Devil didn't hurt Penelope. Instead, she stopped millimeters from the mini pig and reached up to sniff her tentatively before licking her.

Penelope looked to be in hog heaven, pardon the pun. Her little eyes were scrunched closed, the muscles in her cheeks relaxed as an almost purr-like noise emanated from where she stood. I couldn't believe my eyes.

Carefully, I walked towards them, crossing my fingers and hoping Penelope would follow. Looking behind me, Penelope walked, head erect and tail circling wildly, while the She-Beast followed in a bizarre interspecies parade. I got Penelope into her enclosure, but when I tried to grab the cat, it turned into a whirling dervish, scratching, hissing, and biting. Penelope squealed along with the chaos, looking concerned. *Shit.* I couldn't leave the cat behind, no telling what it would do to Albert's home.

Spying a leash and harness hanging on a hook in the enclosure, I held it up and jiggled it. "Who wants to go for a walk?" Penelope snorted and squealed, spinning in happy circles, while the She-Demon looked on. Once secured, I walked them to the door, Penelope walking sedately like a proper dog. As soon as I opened the door though, she high-tailed it for my truck, dragging me behind, stronger than her little size indicated. She jumped up and down at the door to my truck, her snorts and squeals blending together in a cacophony of strange little noises.

I tried to drag her back to the house, but she was immovable. Frantically, I looked around. The cat's carrier was still sitting wide open next to the front door, which also stood propped open. Both the cat and the pig were now trying to get into my truck, the cat leaving scratches on the paint of my door.

Looking heavenward and finding no answers, I retraced my steps back inside, grabbed two bags, one marked "Penelope Morning" and the other marked "Penelope Dinner" along with the container that said "Penelope Treats" with a picture of a pig on it, and shut and locked the front door, grabbed the carrier and loaded both the cat and the pig into the truck along with Penelope's food. Quickly texting Albert, he responded:

Penelope LOVES car rides! Thanks for taking such good care of her! :-)

I put my head on the steering wheel, sighing loudly. How had this spiraled out of control so quickly? And what was I going to do with a cat and a pig?

Turning my car towards Waikoloa, a plan formed.

Chapter Twenty Six

SUMMER

Loud yowling interspersed with a snort every other second reached my ears where I stood at the kitchen counter, shoving musubi in my face, my go to comfort food. The noise got louder, and I peeked out the window.

Cole stood next to his truck in the parking lot, a tiny, pink pig's head hanging out of the passenger window, looking down at an adorable black and white kitten. While I watched, the kitten vaulted up Cole's leg and stood on his shoulders. Cole spun around violently, trying to dislodge it.

"Need some help there, big guy?" I asked after opening the door.

"God yes! Get this She-Beast off of me!" he ordered, his voice holding a note of panic.

My shoulders shook as I did my best to hold in my laughter and removed the kitty and cradled it in my arms. Cole looked from the now-purring cat to me, a dumbfounded look on his face. He muttered something under his breath before turning to the sweet piglet sitting demurely on the passenger seat of his truck.

"Meet Penelope," Cole said, pointing at the pig.

"Oh my gosh, what an angel," I crooned at her. Her little tail started twirling wildly and she snorted with excitement when I reached through the window to pet her with my free hand. The kitty leaned over and started licking Penelope's face and my heart melted on the spot.

"Where on Earth did you get a pig?" I asked. "I didn't even know you had a cat."

"The cat and the pig are both new," he said, his eyes bewildered. "I picked up the cat at the harbor yesterday as a cover when some Russian guy caught me snooping around on his boat. Then when I went to visit Albert in the hospital this morning, he asked me to check on his pet pig, but the cat wouldn't leave without the pig and I couldn't leave the She-Devil there to destroy every shred of furniture in Albert's house, so now I'm stuck with both of them," he said, throwing his hands up in the air in frustration.

Purrs vibrated down my arm as I nuzzled the kitty and tried to process everything Cole had just recited. "Did you say Albert? As in Albert the auctioneer guy?"

Cole nodded. "Someone got ahold of him in the parking lot of the Blue Dragon last night and worked him over pretty good."

I froze and squeezed the cat, her screech letting me know she didn't appreciate it. "Oh, sorry, sweetheart," I told her, rubbing my hands down her back to soothe her, and maybe myself a little too.

My eyes found Cole's. "Was it because of us?" I whispered, my throat instantly feeling tight.

Warm compassion shone through his turquoise-blue eyes as they looked at me. "This isn't your fault. Whatever's going on, whatever Albert got tangled up in has nothing to do with you."

A myriad of thoughts raced through my mind. "But if the goons who followed me saw us talking at the Blue Dragon..." My words faded as I thought about it.

"But Mr. Sam said he already knew I wasn't involved, so unless his goons were following Albert, there wouldn't be any reason to care if they saw me talking to him."

"Mr. Sam?" Cole's voice was low, dangerous.

"Auntie Miriam and I went to see him today. Other than warning me to keep my nose out of this, he turned out to be quite nice. He even gave me a number to call in case I ever get in trouble. Is it wrong that I feel kinda cool knowing a Yakuza boss placed me under his protection? Also, I'm pretty sure he and Auntie are hoping to see each other's *art* soon, if you know what I mean," I joked.

Gagging sounds came from Cole. "Please stop. No more. That is not an image I want in my head." I laughed at him as I picked Penelope up out of the truck and set her down, trickles of sweat running down my neck and back from standing in the hot sun.

"Let's get the children out of the sun," I said, pointing to Penelope and the kitty. "What's your cat's name, anyway?"

"It changes from She-Devil to She-Beast, and sometimes to She-Monster," he answered, keeping his distance as the cat tried to swat him.

"Hmmm. Well, that won't work long term. How about Salem?"

"Like the cat on *Sabrina the Teenage Witch*?" he asked, one side of his mouth quirked up at me.

"Maybe," I said, clutching her close, my voice haughty. "I always wanted a cat growing up, but my dad is allergic. I watched that show obsessively and decided if I ever got a cat, I would name it Salem."

"You know the cat's a girl, right?" he asked.

"Salem works for either," I retorted, annoyed at him for raining on my parade.

His smirk irritated me, so I veered a little closer to him, letting the cat take another swipe. He jumped out of the way just in time, laughing at me.

Once inside, I filled a plastic bowl with water and set it down for the newly named Salem and Penelope. Their little bodies crowded around the bowl; their noses touched first before both took dainty sips.

"What are you doing?" Cole asked as he watched me snap photos of the two with my phone. I got down low, the floor cool on my knees as I shot a photo aimed up at the two little critters.

"I'm getting photos for Insta, what does it look like I'm doing?" I scrolled through my camera roll, looking at what I'd shot before posting. "Elliot's going to flip out. He loves mini pigs." Sure enough, my phone pinged with a message from Elliot.

Don't let them leave—I'm on my way home right now!

I grabbed a can of sparkling water from the refrigerator and held one up to Cole, eyebrow quirked in question.

Nodding, he grabbed the can and popped it open, his Adam's apple bobbing up and down as he took a long swallow. Involuntarily, I stepped closer to him, watching, mesmerized. He caught my eye and stopped mid-swallow.

He set the can down on the counter with exaggerated care and slipped an arm around my waist. "If you keep looking at me like that, I'm going to be forced to kiss you senseless," he warned, his tone deep and persuasive.

My body tingled and I stepped even closer, closing the distance as I tipped my head up. His pupils dilated and his gaze narrowed, voice gravelly when he said, "I warned you."

Fireworks went off in my brain when his lips touched mine, my body wrapping around his of its own accord.

Thump!

We both jumped apart, Cole still holding me close as we watched Elliot nudge the door open with his foot, arms full of grocery bags.

Elliot's eyes tracked to us, taking in Cole's arm wrapped around me, when Penelope snorted and squealed. He set the bags down hastily before bending down to pet the little pig. He cooed at Penelope as she wrapped around him, Salem following suit.

While Elliot was distracted, I tried to pull myself together and get my raging lust under control. Based on the rapid rise and fall of his chest, Cole was doing the same thing. Cole gazed down at me; his attention snagged on my nipples as they loudly announced their interest. He growled and the vibration washed over me. Reluctantly, I stepped away.

Cole was a distraction, and as much as a part of me wanted to revel in that distraction, I needed to stay focused on finding the killer so Lani could come home.

"Wait!" I blurted. "You said a Russian guy busted you at the harbor?" All of my circuits had been scrambled but a few were starting to come back online.

Elliot lifted his head, confused. "Huh?"

"No, not you. Cole. He told me a Russian guy at the harbor caught him snooping around his boat yesterday."

We both looked up expectantly at Cole.

"Yeah. The boat slip mentioned in the note said Slip 2, but it was empty. The slip next to his caught my attention when I noticed some scratch marks and fabric the same color as Wainright's shirt caught in the railing."

"What did the Russian guy look like?" I asked, fear and excitement both vying for attention.

Cole looked at me oddly, but answered my question. His description matched exactly the guy that sought me out at the Beach Club.

"That sounds like the Russian guy staying at the Fairmont!" Elliot said, his voice excited.

Cole stiffened. "Wait here," he ground out, before disappearing through the front door. Elliot and I watched through the window as he grabbed a backpack out of his truck and came back inside.

When he returned, he pulled out his laptop and tapped a few buttons before spinning it around towards Elliot and me.

"That him?" he asked.

I met his eyes above the computer and nodded, then looked at Elliot, his eyes round as saucers. *Shit.*

Chapter Twenty Seven

COLE

RUSSIAN OLIGARCH LANDS IN HAWAII WITH A SPLASH!

Underneath the headline, there was a photo of the man from the harbor sitting behind the wheel of his shiny golden dayboat, surrounded by women in tiny bikinis. The blurb underneath the picture alluded to possible shady dealings in the London financial market.

This was not good. The anxious look on Summer's face echoed my own concerns. I watched as she gulped, a tinge of fear in her eyes, looking away quickly when I turned towards her. I reached out and squeezed her hand; I saw what she tried to cover up with bravado.

"What does this mean?" she asked. "Do you think he had Albert attacked?"

Elliot rubbed her back as he asked, "Is there any evidence this guy was at the auction?"

I cradled my chin in my hand. *Shit.* As much as I didn't want either Elliot or Summer to freak out, I knew they deserved the truth.

"His name showed in the financial records of the auction. All participants are required to show proof of funds in order to take part. Other than Wainright, he had the highest cap."

"Is there any proof he bid on the Lei o mano?" Summer asked. "He seemed really interested in Wainright's body when he questioned me on the beach."

More questions than answers floated through my head, and I did my best to look at this logically. My problem was the list of players involved and all the pieces that didn't seem to fit neatly inside the puzzle.

"I can check with Albert, if he's willing to talk. After last night I can imagine he might have some reservations about sharing any information about the auction."

Summer looked thoughtful. "Do you think it would help if I came with you to talk to him? He seemed to like me when I talked to him at the bar last night."

I shrugged. "It couldn't hurt." I looked down at Penelope as she wrapped herself around Elliot's leg, Salem the cat making wider circles around the two of them like a shark circling prey. Summer followed my gaze.

"Do you think they'd be okay here alone?" she asked. Vehemently I shook my head, picturing Summer and Elliot's furniture after the cat got ahold of it.

"No way. Not if you value your furniture." We both turned to look at Elliot as he cradled the two, murmuring incoherent words to them.

"What? You're not leaving me here. We are the three amigos."

I snorted. "More like the three stooges." A massive sigh gusted through me and I looked up at the ceiling. While I tried to pretend I had control over this investigation, if I was being honest with myself, it was slowly spiraling out of control. *Fuck it.*

"Okay, everyone in the truck," I ordered. Summer and Elliot each grabbed an animal, Summer the cat and Elliot the pig, and we trooped out to my truck like some wild parade of freaks. I muttered to myself the entire way.

"What was that?" Summer asked sweetly, the look on her face amused.

"Nothing," I ground out, grabbing for the limited amount of patience I had left.

Our drive to Waimea soothed my ragged nerves. I put my favorite Island music radio station on and we all sang along to Michael Franti and Bob Marley. By the time I parked at the hospital my frame of mind had improved. I knew allowing Summer and Elliot into the investigation was against HPD rules, but so was fraternizing with the Yakuza. If necessary, I'd play that card.

Summer and I left Elliot out in the truck with the animals and checked in at the front desk again. The same nurse came to the front, eyeing us both up and down. "You're back again," she said flatly.

"He's doing a little better, don't upset him," she ordered as she led us back down the hallway towards Albert's room.

"This shouldn't take long," I reassured the nurse before knocking on Albert's open door.

Albert laid in the same position as before, staring at the television on the wall. When he noticed us, he perked up.

"Hey, Cole. How's Penelope?" he asked. I watched his eyes go wide when he noticed Summer standing slightly behind me. "You're the girl from last night!"

Summer looked down at the floor and I felt her embarrassment as she lifted her head and made eye contact with him, nodding almost imperceptibly.

"Yeah. That was me," her voice quiet.

"You look different," he said, a note of disappointment in his tone.

"This is Summer. Albert, we need to talk to you, and some of this is going to upset you." His gaze sharpened, and I could see how people might underestimate him.

"Go ahead," he said, resigned.

Summer and I laid out the investigation so far, as well as most of what we knew, holding back some details until I knew he could be trusted. He tracked everything, interjecting with shrewd questions before asking one of his own.

I watched a variety of emotions cross his face before eventually he seemed to come to a decision. He nodded to himself before speaking.

"There were several hot ticket items in the auction that drew people in certain circles, the Lei o mano being one of them. Wainright along with Sampo Yamaguchi and Vladimir Demyan all wanted it. To be honest, I was surprised that the bid went to Wainright. When his body turned up, I wasn't really surprised. All of them had deep pockets, but only two of them had the muscle to take what they wanted, if you get my drift."

Several things clicked into place for me at Albert's words. While Wainright was certainly wealthy, the financials I'd examined of the other two men involved showed an even greater amount of wealth. Certainly enough to outbid Wainright.

"So if they couldn't buy the Lei o mano, they would just take it?" Summer questioned.

Albert nodded stiffly at Summer, his eyes shuttering away from her almost instantly. Summer moved closer to Albert's bed and gently grasped his hand.

"I'm sorry for last night's ruse, I truly am. My friend Lani is in big trouble with whoever killed Wainright and I'm desperate to help Cole find them before they find Lani." Sincerity rang out in her voice. At first Albert stiffened and looked away but seemed to soften and turned his head towards her, eyes full of understanding.

Before he could reply, the nurse poked her head in. "Time's up," she stated, looking at the clock pointedly.

I saw Summer squeeze his hand and then turn towards the nurse in the doorway. "Is he allowed to have Penelope come say hello really quickly?" she asked.

"We only allow two visitors at a time, so one of you will have to leave," she answered, looking directly at me.

Summer's eyes traveled between the two of us, the beginnings of a smirk on her face. "Cole doesn't mind waiting in the truck, do you, Cole?" she looked at me, eyes filled with laughter.

"No, that's fine," I answered, my look full of retribution as I stared at Summer.

The nurse nodded in satisfaction just as we heard an overhead page. "Code Stroke, ETA five minutes. Code Stroke, ETA five minutes."

"Just let the unit secretary know I okayed another visitor for Albert," the nurse called as she ran towards the ambulance bay at the back of the unit.

I watched as Summer took Penelope's leash from Elliot and went back through the sliding glass doors, gesturing towards the back as she spoke to the unit secretary. She disappeared through the double doors towards Albert's room, and I had to shake my head while simultaneously marveling at her audacity.

Chapter Twenty Eight

SUMMER

ALBERT SEEMED TO APPRECIATE Penelope's visit, thanking me profusely, which went a long way to assuage my guilt at my deception last night.

"Can you keep her a few more nights until they release me?" he asked, anxiety filling his voice.

"Of course. Cole's cat Salem is in love with Penelope, and I think it's mutual," I answered.

Albert wrinkled his nose. "Hmm. Detective Peterson doesn't strike me as a cat person."

I laughed. "I don't think he was, but he is now—whether or not he likes it." I filled Albert in on the story Cole told us about Salem.

Albert laughed, but then winced in pain and froze. I squeezed his hand and Penelope tried to jump on the bed, sensing his distress.

"I'm so sorry this happened to you. You didn't deserve it." My heart thumped painfully seeing this real–life character look so diminished laying in his hospital bed.

He waved away my words as he caught his breath. He closed his eyes briefly, seeming to gather his strength. Albert squeezed my hand back.

"Summer, please be careful. The men involved in Wainright's murder are very dangerous, and they don't play games. If they think you have what they want, they will stop at nothing to take it from you. My biggest regret is not getting out of that world before this happened."

I nodded and lifted Penelope up so he could say goodbye before heading back out to Cole's truck.

Elliot sensed how upset I was. He rubbed my back comfortingly and murmured, "She's safe on the mainland." Leave it to him to cut right to the heart of my fear. Cole watched the byplay between us. He looked like he wanted to ask questions, but swallowed them before ushering us back into the truck.

"Wanna grab something at the drive-thru?" he asked, pointing at a McDonald's on the corner. I wrinkled my nose and made retching noises, while Elliot's mouth dropped open in horror.

"Umm, no thank you," Elliot said primly, "we prefer to eat actual food not designed to kill us."

Irritation flashed across Cole's face briefly before he capitulated. "Fair. What do you suggest?"

Elliot volunteered to cook carbonara for us, so Cole swung into the Foodland parking lot, and we waited with Salem and Penelope while he ran in to grab ingredients.

Back at home, we fed the animals and offered Elliot our assistance, which he rejected as the empty offer it was, so we watched him cook while we drank wine and speculated about Wainright's murderer.

"So, if Mr. Sam is in the clear, then it has to be the Russian dude, Demyan, that did it, right?" Elliot asked as he deftly whisked ingredients together in the cast-iron skillet on the stove.

Secretly, I hoped that was the case. Even though I sensed Mr. Sam was capable of some pretty hardcore things, I wanted to believe he was innocent in this case. Cole squashed that hope when he replied.

"Not necessarily. From what Summer found out today he also wants the Lei o mano and the pendant, meaning he didn't take it from Wainright. But that doesn't exclude him from being guilty of murdering Wainright to get what he wanted."

Elliot and I looked at each other sideways, guilt written all over our faces. I liked Cole. Alot. But I wasn't ready to give up Lani to help him with this case. There's no telling what kind of trouble she would get into for having a mur-der weapon in her possession and no witnesses to prove her innocence. The only way that I could see Lani getting off without jail time was to get a full confession from the murderer. Or at least finding enough evidence to point away from her.

"Kobayashi Maru," Elliot said to me, reading my mind. Cole's gaze sharpened as he looked first at Elliot, then at me.

"Care to explain?" he asked, his voice low, suspicion vi-brating off of him in waves.

I waved my hand at him airily. "Oh, nothing. Just a little Star Trek reference." I hoped he wasn't a fan, otherwise he'd know we were hiding something.

"Yes, I'm familiar. What exactly is the no-win situation here?"

Shit, Shit, Shit. Thankfully, Elliot jumped in the void to answer for me. I was a terrible liar, my poker face virtually non-existent.

"Summer's worried about Auntie Miriam's love interest and doesn't want to get caught up in the middle and face her wrath," he answered. My head whipped towards him, my eyes widened in surprise. How had he found out about Auntie and Mr. Sam? I hadn't said a word about it to him.

"Coconut telegraph," he mouthed to me when Cole bent down to pick up Penelope. Ahh, of course.

"So, what are you going to do with Penelope?" I asked Cole, hoping to change the subject.

He looked down and blew out a breath. Salem was trying to climb up his leg to get to Penelope. He set the pig down abruptly and took a step away from them.

He lifted his shoulders and then shrugged. "I don't know. I feel like this entire investigation, and everything involved has spiraled out of control to where I'm just reacting and not planning."

I laughed. "Welcome to my world. To my life if I'm being honest." While I loved the *idea* of planning things out and being organized, things seldom worked out that way for me.

Elliot cleared his throat and we both turned in his direction. "Far be it from me to involve myself in your business..."

I rolled my eyes at this. Elliot involved himself in *every-one's* business like he was practicing to be a professional yenta.

"But what about if you stay here, at least for tonight? Salem and Penelope seem comfortable here, and I for one would feel better having an officer of the law here in case anyone tries to come after Summer."

My mind strayed to the kiss we'd shared earlier. I crossed my heart I would stay away from Cole romantically, at least until we cleared Lani's name. Having him under our roof might be too much temptation to resist.

One look at Cole's face and I could tell he was thinking along the same lines. I watched his Adam's apple bob up and down as he swallowed nervously before answering.

"Uh, sure. I don't have a litter box or anything for Salem, though." My heart, and parts down lower melted. I was a sucker for a man who made responsible decisions. *I must be getting old.*

"No problem," Elliot chirped. "Our neighbor has all kinds of cat paraphernalia. She's always feeding the stray cats around here. I'll just run over and borrow some stuff."

I watched in dismay as Elliot slid out the front door. My heart sped up. Just being near Cole was proving difficult to resist. I watched as Penelope rubbed against his leg. Was I wrong for being jealous of a pig?

"Summer." Cole growled; his voice low, desperate.

Naked desire showed on his face, likely a match to mine. Oh lord, tonight was going to be a long night...

Chapter Twenty Nine

COLE

I SPENT A LONG, restless night on Summer's couch for the second night in a row, doing my best not to picture Summer laying upstairs in her bed, wondering what she was wearing, wondering if she was replaying our interrupted kiss in her head like I was.

I gave up trying to sleep by the time the sun peeked over Mauna Kea and its rays filtered through the front window. I looked over to where Penelope and Salem lay curled up together on a pile of old blankets that Elliot had brought over from their neighbor, little mewls and snores coming from their direction. Tiptoeing past them into the kitchen, I found the coffeemaker and rummaged around for some coffee beans.

Coffee percolated and hissed into the coffee pot while I watched impatiently. I filled a cup the second the machine beeped at me and took a scalding hot swallow while heading to the bathroom. My reflection in the mirror above the sink showed a five o'clock shadow and bleary, bloodshot eyes. I splashed cold water on my face, hoping that would help.

Frustrated with myself, I went over where exactly I'd lost control of the investigation. I knew I'd crossed professional boundaries in more ways than one with Summer and Elliot, for which I had no logical explanation. Something about Summer, and by extension, Elliot, led me to share more than what was proper from the get-go. While I could blame part of it on my attraction to Summer, a larger part of it came from sensing her honest desire to help find the killer. Even if she was holding something back about Lani's whereabouts, my gut told me she was sincere and innocent of any involvement with Wainright's murderer.

Last night when Elliot mentioned the phrase Kobayashi Maru, I'd detected something more than Auntie Miriam's involvement with Mr. Sam as their chief concern. If I was being honest with myself, my feelings had been a little bruised. After spending so much time with them in such a short period I had felt like part of the gang, but last night a distinct wall went up between the three of us.

Meowing from the living room drew my attention and I saw Salem the cat nudging Penelope's food bowl with her nose, Penelope's jerky movements and soft snorts alerting me to the fact that I hadn't kept up on the strict feeding schedule Albert gave me.

Letting out a pent-up breath and running my hand through my tangled hair, I grabbed the container of Penelope's food and filled her bowl before doing the same for Salem. Little crunching and chortling noises sounded as they ate, and I had to admit they made a cute, if slightly odd, duo. I had no idea how I was going to care for both of them until Albert got out of the hospital, and judging by their behavior, I didn't think I'd be able to split them up. *Shit.*

After they were done eating, I took Penelope out to do her business, Salem following us. I half-heartedly hoped Salem would run off, but she stayed glued to Penelope's side.

Summer was walking down the stairs just as we came back in, her skimpy sleep shorts and tank top causing my heart rate to increase and other parts of me to stand up and take notice. She brushed by me to grab coffee with a mumble, and the clean, ocean scent of her shampoo sent me into overdrive as much as her nearness. I gritted my teeth and clenched my hands to prevent myself from reaching for her.

"Good morning," I said as I watched her chug half the mug of coffee in one go. She just nodded before downing the rest of it and pouring another cup. The fact that she was cranky too lifted my spirits and I grinned at her.

"What?" she demanded, her tone irritated, causing my grin to stretch even wider.

"Nothing." I shrugged my shoulders and lifted my hands, palms up, doing my best to hide my grin from her. "How'd you sleep?" I asked.

"Grrr..." she responded. At that, I laughed outright, earning a dirty look from Summer.

Elliot picked that moment to come down the stairs whistling. We both looked at him as he jauntily crossed through the kitchen, heading towards the coffeepot.

"So, what's on tap for today?" he asked, his tone breezy.

I looked over at Summer. "Is he always this annoyingly cheerful in the morning?" She nodded.

"Oh, now, come on. Some of us just sleep better than others, especially when we aren't thinking carnal thoughts all night." Tongue in cheek, he started whistling, and I was pretty sure I was going to have to strangle him.

"Urrrggghhhh!" Summer threw up her hands and then stomped back up the stairs.

My eyes tracked her every movement, appreciating the sway of her backside as she went. Elliot caught me looking and threw a dishtowel at my head. I grinned, unrepentant, and he just shook his head and smiled before pouring himself a cup of coffee.

Elliot made breakfast burritos for all of us, the bacon perfectly crispy and the addition of Hawaiian peppers adding a spicy little kick.

"Dude, if I was gay, I'd totally marry you," I declared just as Summer walked back down the stairs, this time clothed in green cargo shorts that set off her tan and a white T-shirt with the image of a humpback whale and the Kohala Divers logo on it.

"Too late, I already called dibs," Summer announced.

Elliot tucked his chin to the side, but I saw a small, satisfied smile on his face.

Summer bent down and picked Salem up and snuggled the black and white cat before she asked, "What's the plan for today?" echoing Elliot's earlier question.

"I want to go into the precinct today and talk to the officer who's worked on a few international cases and get his take on some of this. Then I want to look more into our Russian friend and see what I can dredge up. The only problem is Salem and Penelope. I don't think I can manage both of them and get any work done." I looked at Summer and Elliot, my eyes hopeful.

Summer snuggled Salem closer, looking into the cat's slanted green eyes, "We can take care of you, can't we, sweet girl? You want to stay with Summer and snuggle?" she crooned, stroking the cat's fur and holding her against her breasts.

I don't think I've envied an animal more than I did in that moment.

"Don't forget the catering gig tonight," Elliot reminded Summer.

"Oh, that's right." Summer looked up at the ceiling as if accessing some internal database before she turned to me.

"I can ask our neighbor Deb if she can keep an eye on them if you're not back before we leave." She tilted her head at me in question while sinking her face into Sabrina's fur.

Just then, my phone started playing the theme song to *Star Wars*. I glanced at the screen and let out an accidental groan. I sent it to voicemail, feeling Elliot and Summer's eyes on me, curiosity written plainly on their faces.

My pocket vibrated, and the song played again, and I closed my eyes, praying for patience as I pulled the phone out of my pocket.

"Hey, Ma," I said through gritted teeth.

Chapter Thirty
SUMMER

Elliot and I watched Cole as he talked to his mom on the phone, the myriad expressions on his face amusing to watch. After several long-suffering sighs and "yes, ma's", I heard him ask if she could babysit Salem and Penelope overnight and my ears perked up. What did Cole have to do overnight that he needed to get rid of the fur babies? I tried not to let myself get too lost in theories, but jealousy gnawed at my stomach.

When he hung up, he announced his mom had agreed to take Salem and Penelope until tomorrow morning.

"Oh, okay. Are you sure? We wouldn't mind keeping them." I said, watching his face closely.

"I'll be paying for it for weeks, but she agreed. Apparently, her 'allergies'," he made air quotes, "are mild enough she can take Salem for a short time. I'm starting to think she never had allergies in the first place—she just told me that so I wouldn't pester her for a pet." He shook his head. "What a shyster. Well, anyway, I'll text Albert to let him know," he said, spinning around and tapping a message on his phone.

I was dying to know what he had going on tonight but was too stubborn to ask. Elliot smirked at me and I flipped him the bird behind my back. I debated whether or not to tell him that the party I was working at the Fairmont was for the Russian guy, Demyan. On the one hand, I felt like he should know, but on the other hand, I didn't want him to interfere with my snooping. Before I could decide, he stood up to leave.

"Well, I'm going to head out so I can drop these guys off and see what I can find out about the Russian." With that, he saluted, loaded up the animals, and left.

Elliot left shortly after, reminding me to be at the Fairmont at three for the banquet. I nodded absentmindedly, still wondering where Cole was going to be tonight that he needed his mom to watch the animals.

"Urrrrgghh," I muttered, frustrated with myself. What did it matter? Cole and I weren't dating. He was free to do whatever, or whomever, he chose. I didn't have to like it, though.

Slamming the dishes into the dishwasher and yanking the trash out from under the sink, I stomped outside to the dumpster and threw it in with more force than I probably needed to. As I crossed the parking lot back to the house, I spied Mr. Sam's lackeys sitting in the parking lot. When we made eye contact, they tried to duck down, and I flipped them off. Fuming, I angrily texted Mr. Sam once I got back inside the condo. He replied with a smiley face emoji and said they were there for my protection.

I muttered to myself while I finished cleaning the condo, a job I had left on the back burner for far too long if the layers of dust were any indication. I blared my unhinged Spotify playlist while I cleaned, doing my best to keep my mind off of Cole and our non-existent relationship.

When it came time to leave for the banquet, I looked around in satisfaction at the sparkling clean condo. The smell of lemon wafted throughout, and every surface was cleared off. Elliot sent me heart emojis when I told him I'd done all the laundry too.

I guess a good mad was good for something, I thought to myself as I unlocked my car and headed down to the Fairmont. Dumb and Dumber tailed behind me, but to their credit, they were getting better at not being so obvious.

Elliot was waiting for me in the open-air lobby, the ocean serving as a stunning backdrop to the marble floors and pillars. I'd always loved this hotel. Memories of staying here when I was little welled up inside me. Learning how to paddleboard and going out with the beach boys on the outrigger canoe is what convinced me I was going to be the next Eddie Aikou. Looking for turtles along the shoreline at night. My face softened at the memories.

Elliot snapped his fingers in front of my face, bringing me back to the present. "Follow me." he said, his tone curt.

I wondered what could have caused this shift. Once he punched the button for the service level on the elevator and the door closed, he turned to me, his face serious.

"I overheard two of the guys with Demyan talking. I think they have the pendant." He handed me a key card and a slip of paper with a code on it.

"This is the master key to get into their room and the universal code for the safe. If anyone finds out you have this, not only will I lose my job, but we'll both end up in jail."

"Elliot, how did you get this?" I asked, worried he'd lose his job.

"It involved a lot of flirting with the security guard and offering to watch the security cameras while he went to grab lunch. He stores all the room key doubles in a safe that he keeps unlocked when he's working."

My mind whirled, not even wanting to consider the repercussions if we got caught. "Wait—what about the code?"

He dismissed my question with a wave of his hand. "Easy. They all have the same universal code. It hasn't changed for five years."

My heart stuttered, then sped up as I looked at the card in my hand. I held the chance to exonerate Lani and uncover the killers in my hand. My hands shook, but my voice was steady when I responded. "Let's do this."

Chapter Thirty One

COLE

Penelope snorted excitedly as my mom snuggled her, the cat rubbing against her leg. Mom lifted her eyes to me, an expression of adoration in them. *Phew.* I dragged in all the stuff and set it up in the corner my mom pointed me to, all the while thinking about the case.

Mr. Sam couldn't be removed from the list of suspects, but it was looking less and less likely that he had any involvement in the murder. Demyan seemed the most likely culprit, but good detective work required thoughtful, thorough investigation and not jumping to conclusions. The problem for me was that if Demyan had anything to do with Wainright's murder, then Elliot and Summer were heading into a hornet's nest of danger tonight. The only reason I knew about tonight was because Elliot let it slip last night. I tried to shove down the hurt that Summer hadn't mentioned it to me. She was a tough, independent woman, but she was playing with fire. And as much as I believed Summer could handle herself, Demyan had the upper hand.

"Got a hot date tonight?" my mom asked, her tone casual, but her eyes were bright with interest.

"In a manner of speaking," I replied, not willing to elaborate.

She just nodded and I headed out the door. "I'll come by in the morning sometime to pick up the beasts," I told her.

"They're not beasts. Look at this sweet baby." My mom held Salem out to me and Salem's eyes narrowed with malice as she swiped at me, growling. I glared at her and then kissed my mom's cheek as she held the She-Beast out of the way.

"Stupid cat," I muttered as I walked to my truck. Checking the time, I figured I'd have just enough time to go home and shower before running to the office and checking with my contacts regarding Demyan.

Chapter Thirty Two

COLE

"HEY, PETERSON. LONG TIME no see." Jack Hall, our department's FBI contact, reached out to shake my hand, his grip strong. He motioned to the seat across from him, and I took a moment to look around at the bustling coffee shop before I sat.

"Hey, man. Thanks for meeting with me on such short notice. How've you been?"

We caught up with each other, Jack pulling out his phone to show me pictures from his daughter's recent wedding.

"Thank God she looks like her mom," I ribbed him.

"Ain't that the truth—" He scratched his head of graying hair, his blue eyes twinkling.

"So what's up? Your message sounded mysterious," he asked as he sipped from the mug in front of him.

After updating him on the case so far, he let out a long whistle. "Demyan's bad news, buddy. If he's involved, tread carefully. He's the prime suspect in more than half a dozen crimes across the globe, but somehow always avoids prosecution."

He pulled something up on his phone, then slid it over to me. I noticed him casually checking the area with an air of studied indifference, but I knew better. Jack was the best in the field. His non-descript appearance belied a brilliant mind underneath.

I slid the phone back over after I read the case reports. I tried for nonchalance when I asked Jack what he thought Demyan was capable of, but my voice dipped slightly as a picture of Summer came to mind.

Jack sensed my growing concern, his eyes grave. "If I were you, I would do everything I could to stay out of his crosshairs. Those crimes I mentioned earlier came with a body count."

Shit. My heart dropped at his words. I thanked him for his time, and he encouraged me to reach out if I needed help on the case. I nodded, my mind distracted with thoughts of Summer and the banquet tonight.

"Cole, I'm serious—count me in if you find anything. I'd love to get this guy behind bars before I retire. Reach out if you need anything, okay? I'll bend whatever rules I can without breaking them to make it happen."

Jack's words stayed with me as I drove back up north to the Fairmont. Finding Wainright's killer took a backseat to keeping Summer safe as far as I was concerned. I just wasn't sure if Summer would feel the same way. As I threw my truck keys to the valet and made my way through the lobby, I kept my senses tuned for any hint of danger, acutely aware that Summer might not appreciate my interference with her plans for tonight.

Chapter Thirty Three

SUMMER

"Ouch!" The ribbing on the corset stabbed my side and I thought about throwing it in the trash. Elliot had warned me that Demyan had demanded we all wear matching uniforms—if you could call them that. The women were handed grass skirts that barely covered our asses, the tops a facsimile of a coconut bra, the corset made from real coconuts, for that oh so 'authentic' feel. I rolled my eyes at the thought.

The men were given loincloths, many opting to wear boxer's underneath. I took a moment to rail at the injustice of it all. At least they would be comfortable. I'd be tugging my corset up and my skirt down all night just to make sure everything stayed covered.

The good news was that my irritation with our uniforms was keeping me from freaking out about breaking in and looking for the pendant in Demyan's room. In the back of my mind, I catalogued all the ways I could screw this up.

And these stupid uniforms had almost no room for me to hide the key card. If I was a little less well-endowed, I could at least put it in my bra, but as it was, I had to keep a close eye on the girls to make sure they didn't escape.

My phone vibrated on the sink counter. A text from Elliot:

Keep your phone on you. I'll let you know when the coast is clear.

I looked down at my barely-there uniform. I was going to have to get creative fitting the keycard and my phone in. I managed to wedge both inside the bra, but the fallout was it created a gap in my cleavage. *Shit.*

A line of servers snaked through the door to the terraced banquet area on the sixth floor. A tall, darkly handsome man with cold brown eyes watched us as we walked through, giving each of us a cold, clinical assessment. *Were they looking for weapons?* I wondered.

Aside from the guests, who were easy to pick out given their high-end designer clothes and fawning over the man taking center stage in the terrace's corner, I tracked at least three other bodyguards. Although they were dressed similarly to the guests, their watchfulness and serious demeanor made them easy to pick out. As I watched, two of the guards flanked Demyan, hands in front of their bodies, the slight bulge underneath their clothes a telltale sign they were carrying.

I did my best not to draw any attention to myself, since Demyan would likely recognize me. While I filled, and plated, and smiled, my mind strayed to how best to get into Demyan's room without being seen. What I needed was a diversion.

Just then, a loud crash drew everyone's attention, and I watched as a young server scrambled to pick up the platter of pupus knocked out of her hand by the wildly gesticulating white haired man in a loud aloha shirt. HIs lascivious grin as she bent over to pick up the mess had my hands balling into fists.

Punching guests is bad, punching guests is bad. The words ran like a mantra in my head until I felt my fists unclench. I made a mental note of the man though in case I ever ran into him outside of the Fairmont.

The banquet had been laid out lavishly, but casually. Plenty of food covered all available surfaces, and the dinner itself was buffet style. This allowed me to circulate, refilling glasses and removing plates while staying alert to the opportunity to sneak away and search Demyan's room across the hall. I'd noticed two guards standing on either side of his door earlier. Whatever diversion I came up with, it better be good.

Once the dinner was cleared away and dessert stations were set up, music played. Quiet at first, then with increasing volume, a haunting Hawaiian song played on a single ukelele. From a side door, Jake Shimabukuro walked out, strumming his ukelele and crooning softly. The crowd quieted as they watched the master at work.

Everyone in the room stood rapt, listening. The bodyguards seemed unaffected, but I caught one with a dreamy look on his face, swaying slightly. I didn't know if this would be enough of a distraction to pull the guards' attention away from what I needed to do.

Demyan's attention diverted away from the virtuoso in front of him to something on his right, and as I watched, a Bengal tiger was brought in, a sparkling, diamond encrusted collar surrounding its massive neck. The handler gave Demyan the end of the leash with a respectful bow before moving out of the way. The tiger stood next to Demyan, quivering occasionally as Demyan ran his hands down the tiger's back.

Demyan stood up and so did the tiger, eerily mirroring his master's movements as they stalked toward Jake Shimabukuro. Jake's face shifted slightly, his eyes drawn to the tiger as Demyan stood next to him, silently showing dominance. Jake's nose twitched, then crinkled, his face turning red right before he started sneezing. The sneeze startled the tiger who leaped sideways, pulling Demyan with him. Jake, terrified, jumped as well, crashing into the microphone stand and speaker, the screech echoing painfully throughout the room. Bodyguards scrambled to get to Demyan.

I looked around at the mayhem. This was it. Just then, my phone vibrated under my coconut bra, and I watched the guards from Demyan's private quarters rush in. Sidling out, keeping my eyes on the guards, I rushed across the empty hallway and jammed the keycard against the door. Shutting it quickly behind me, I took a moment to gaze at the opulence in front of me before searching for the safe.

Luckily, I'd worked small dinner parties in the past. Rooms were laid out pretty similarly, and I found the safe in the closet nestled between the main room and the master bathroom. Punching in the code Elliot gave me, my heart pounded as I prayed it would work. The light turned green, and the door swung open.

Inside, among several expensive-looking necklaces and watches, was a plain black jewelry box. Nestled within was a shark tooth pendant. The cords wrapped around it were ancient-looking, a sparkling blue stone that glowed eerily was nestled in the center.

I held it up to the dim light, watching as the blue stone lit up and shined outward. Fascinated, I held the pendant against my neck, mesmerized. A noise startled me and I dropped the pendant and watched as it snagged on my top. Trying to dislodge only caused it to get more stuck. Just as one end broke free, a hand wrapped around my mouth, a rock-hard body pressing tightly against me.

Chapter Thirty Four

COLE

Summer's scantily clad body pressed against my chest did funny things to me, and my mind went blank. Her squirming didn't help any, either.

"Shhh," I whispered. Her squirming stopped, but just as I let my guard down, she surged upwards, catching my nose with the top of her head.

"Ow!" I muttered, checking for blood. Summer's eyes widened in surprise before narrowing. She smacked me, hard.

"You scared me to death, you idiot!"

I held my nose and did my best not to let my eyes stray downwards. Blood spurted from where she'd made contact and she grabbed the nearest thing, a scarf that looked like it cost more than my yearly salary, and clasped it against my nose as she squeezed.

"Theguardsarebackinplace," I said.

"What?" she asked; my words so jumbled even I wasn't sure what I'd said.

I pulled back a couple inches. "I said the guards are back in place. Unless we jump off the sixth–floor balcony, there's no way out." I watched as her eyes narrowed in concentration, pacing in the narrow space. She reached down into her coconut bra and wiggled something shiny before groaning in frustration. My interest in escape plummeted the farther down her hand went. Other parts of me cheered. Just as things were getting really interesting, she pulled a cell phone out and tapped on the screen. A second later, it buzzed and she looked up at me.

"Elliot's going to signal me. We'll have about 1.2 seconds at best to get out of here without getting caught."

I brought my attention back where it belonged and nodded sharply.

Silently we crept to the front door, standing just behind it. Summer's face looked pale and serious in the sliver of moonlight that shone on our hiding spot. Reaching over, I squeezed her hand, and she kept it, holding on to it like a lifeline as we waited. Just when I was convinced the signal wasn't coming, I felt the vibration from Summer's phone.

She glanced at the screen and gestured to the door. I grabbed her and swung her just outside the door and a few steps away when a guard emerged from the terrace across the hall. I hid my face from view, but out of the corner of my eye I saw him observe us, a suspicious look on his face.

Taking matters into my own hands, I pressed Summer up against the wall and kissed her. Her eyes went wide in protest, but I kept kissing her, running my hands down her body in a way I'd been itching to do since I met her.

The guard snorted as Summer finally caught on. She made little whimpering cries, noises of appreciation. "Ohhhh...." And even though I knew she was just acting, I couldn't help but get swept up in it, pouring everything I had into that kiss.

Dimly, I heard another man walk nearby, addressing the guard. "Situation's handled," he said succinctly, then, "What's this?"

His comrade answered, "Apparently they couldn't wait to get a room." Crude laughter sounded in my ears and then I felt a none too gentle nudge in my ribcage.

"Move on. This is a private area, not part of the party." I lifted my head no more than an inch and nodded, then swung Summer around in front of me so they couldn't see her face as we walked down the hallway. I was thankful she walked in front of me, as my raging hard on tented my jeans and made it hard to walk.

As we rounded the corner near the elevators, a hand snaked out and grabbed Summer, pulling her into the supply closet. I slammed my hand against the door before it could close completely, ready to tear apart anyone who tried to hurt her.

Elliot's eyes rounded as he looked first at me, and then at Summer, then back again, his mouth agape. I would've laughed at the comical look on his face if I weren't trying frantically to calm down the lower parts of me.

"What happened?" he asked Summer, then looked at me. Summer reached into her bra again, doing nothing to help my current situation, and after a brief struggle, pulled out a fragile-looking pendant in the shape of a shark's tooth, the bone glistening iridescent, almost seeming to glow from within.

Elliot squawked, then covered his mouth. "You got it! I can't believe it!"

Chapter Thirty Five

SUMMER

"Yep." Even to me my voice sounded hoarse and shaky. I shook my head and tried again. "I got it. Now–what do we do with it?"

Cole cleared his throat behind me, and Elliot and I both turned to face him. His flushed cheeks and tangled hair just added to the sex appeal and my lower parts tingled, wanting to go back to what we were doing before.

"You're the popo, what are we supposed to do with it now that we found the necklace? Do you call in your team and arrest Demyan?" Elliot asked.

"First off, popo is so two thousand four. Second, since Summer broke into Demyan's safe to find it, not only would it be inadmissible in a court of law, but Summer could also be arrested," Cole replied, his eyes serious.

"But he did it! Why else would he have the pendant?" Elliot burst out.

I had a sinking feeling as I considered Cole's words. Mental head slap. If I would've left the pendant in the safe, at least it would be in Demyan's possession, and he could be questioned. Especially if someone were to call in an anonymous tip. Shit, shit, shit. I'd totally messed up.

Visions of my dad visiting me in jail ran through my head, my heart pounding in my ears, my mouth dry. My hands shook as I considered the magnitude of my fuck up. Cole placed a comforting arm around my shoulder.

"Here's what we're going to do. Summer, I want you and Elliot to head back to your condo immediately. I'll follow you. Then we're going to come up with a plan for the pendant. We can't return it with all the security in place, too risky." He shrugged his shoulders, "So the next best thing is to figure out where to stash it for now."

Cole's plan was completely reasonable, but I couldn't help but notice a thread of fear in his tone.

I looked down at my outfit. "How am I going to get out of here without drawing attention to myself?" I asked.

Elliot smiled and reached behind him, grabbing one of the environmental services uniforms and handing it to me. "Put this on."

I eyed both Cole and Elliot and ordered them to turn around while I wriggled my way out of the coconut corset, a sigh of relief escaping me as the restrictive top came off.

"Summer..." I heard Cole growl in warning, reminding me what had happened only minutes ago and how small the supply closet was. Elliot smacked the back of Cole's head and gave him stink eye.

Quickly changing and stashing the banquet costume I turned around. "Okay, let's get out of here."

Cole eyed the new clothes and scrunched up his nose, and I punched his arm. "Knock it off," I ordered.

Elliot peeked out of the closet, then motioned for Cole and me. We hightailed it down the service hallway to the parking lot and parted ways. Elliot's car sat in a pool of light cast from the light pole nearby. The closer we got the more sinister every shadow seemed. Just before I reached the car, a hand touched me.

"Gahhh!" I yelled and spun around. Elliot shushed me and kept a hand on my shoulder as we crept closer.

Nothing jumped out at us, and we made it into the car safely and headed out, Elliot driving so fast he almost clipped the automatic gate as we went through. The lights from Foodland were a beacon of sanctuary up ahead. Cole's truck sat parked partially hidden near the giant monkeypod tree in the side parking lot. Elliot drove past, and Cole's truck pulled out and followed us home.

The warm lights from the condo never seemed so inviting as they did when we pulled into the parking lot. The events of the night were catching up to me and my hands and body shook, realizing just how dumb I'd been, the foolish risk I had taken breaking into Demyan's room.

A knock sounded on the window next to my head and I screeched, jumping several inches into the air, my heart immediately racing like I was competing in the 100-meter sprint. Cole stood outside. I grabbed my chest as I rolled the window down.

"Wait out here while I check out the condo," he ordered, holding out his hand. Elliot dutifully handed over the keys to our condo, and we both watched as Cole pulled his service weapon from the holster on his hip. Seeing Cole pull out his gun brought home the seriousness of our situation.

The girl part of me couldn't help but feel a little punch of lust though, as I watched him in action. He slipped into ninja mode as he first checked the door and windows and then let himself inside. My stomach churned with anxiety until he appeared at the doorway several minutes later and waved us in.

Once inside, I changed into sweats, inspecting the deep indents on my sides from the coconut corset. I shook my head. Ony a man would consider a coconut corset a viable costume for a woman.

When I came back downstairs, Elliot handed me a tumbler of whiskey and gestured toward Cole sitting on the couch, staring out the window, looking pensive. I plopped down next to him and held the glass out. He took it and downed it in one swallow, hissing and grimacing as it went down.

He stared over at me and opened his mouth, but before saying anything he looked away again, burying his head in his hands. "This case is totally fucked," he muttered.

His back felt warm and solid under my hand as I rubbed, making bigger circles as I went. Guilt swamped me. A large part of the blame for this screw up lay on my shoulders. Mentally berating myself for my impulsive decision to break into Demyan's room, I attempted to apologize. "I'm so sor—"

"This isn't your fau—" Cole said at the same time.

We both stopped and he gestured for me to go first. "I'm so sorry. I shouldn't have broken into Demyan's room and unintentionally stolen the pendant. It doesn't excuse my behavior, but clearing Lani and getting this guy off her back is my utmost priority and I let it blind me to common sense."

Cole acknowledged my words with a nod. "I get it. I shouldn't have let you guys get involved from the start. Because of my appalling lapse in judgement, for which there is no excuse, Demyan may get off scot free."

My phone vibrated just then.

"My men will drop your car off for you in the morning." "Mr. Sam included a smiley face emoji. Oh vey.

As much as I chafed at being followed and 'protected', if that's what this was, I couldn't help but feel grateful knowing they were watching out for me right now. If Demyan found out I had the pendant, I'd need all the protection I could get.

Chapter Thirty Six

COLE

FOLDED BLANKETS LAY ON the couch when I came out of the bathroom. Summer's remorseful look as she handed me pillows made me feel even worse. Mentally, I berated myself for coming out guns blazing about Lani when I first approached Summer. Maybe if I had handled things differently from the beginning Summer wouldn't have felt that she had to take action on her own.

And, if I was being really honest, I'd already crossed so many lines sharing information and including Summer and Elliot in parts of the investigation. No, Summer wasn't to blame for this fiasco of an investigation. The blame rested squarely on my shoulders. Now I just need to figure out how to unfuck this situation before Demyan got away with murder, or worse, came after Summer.

Thankfully, Summer didn't think Demyan had seen her at the banquet. Hopefully, that was true. As soon as he noticed the missing pendant, he'd be on a warpath to find it, and Summer would be first on the culprit list if he'd noticed her presence.

For the third night in a row, I slept on Summer and Elliot's couch, and other than a slight crick in my neck in the morning I had no complaints. Just before I fell asleep, a picture of Summer wrapped in my arms crossed my mind. The memory of her soft moans and sighs, velvet skin, and addicting scent made it hard for me to sleep, but eventually I drifted off.

The sun's rays were just stretching across the mountain, and I still hadn't figured out what to do to get this investigation back on track, but one thing was certain—I needed to stash the pendant somewhere safe. Visions of what Demyan and his thugs might do to Summer if she were caught with it made my blood run cold.

When I brought it up with Summer, her only answer was a sleepy nod as she ran back up the stairs, then came back down and placed it gently in my hand like the sacred artifact it was.

Summer hesitated, drew in a deep breath and looked to the side, almost shyly, before speaking. "Cole, you're under no obligation, but will you check in with me today and just let me know how things are going?"

I opened my mouth to speak, but she stopped me, holding up a finger. "You don't have to give me details, just a general good, bad, or working on it. What I said last night still stands. Clearing Lani's name and getting Demyan off her back are my priorities."

I nodded, then asked what her plans were for the day.

"I have work. Nothing after that."

She drummed her hand on the counter while she waited for the coffee to finish brewing. She glanced at me from the corner of her eye. "You're welcome to come over for dinner. If you want to." Her voice was stilted, like she was going for casual but that it meant a great deal to her.

"Sure," I said easily.

As I headed out, she called after me, "And bring Penelope and Salem!"

I groaned. I'd completely forgotten about my animal sitting duties. Dammit. This was going to put a kink in my plans. What little plan I'd formed, that was...

When I got to my mom's house, she met me at the door holding Salem. As soon as I came into range, she tried to take a swipe at me, and I leaned back.

My mom eyed me up and down. "Why are you the only person the cat doesn't like?"

I shrugged, but when she wasn't looking, I scowled at the cat. She just flicked her tail at me and turned around. Penelope came running up when she heard my voice and snorted happily at my feet until I picked her up and petted her. At least one beast liked me.

After loading the animals in my truck, I texted Albert to let him know Penelope needed more food. He responded:

Good news. They're discharging me today. Is there any way you can pick me up?

I texted back:

I'd be happy to. You'll have to share your seat with Penelope, though...

I drove over to Waimea and Albert and Nurse Ratched were waiting for us at the front door, Albert held about ten flower arrangements on his lap in the wheelchair they wheeled him out in. I raised an eyebrow and then looked inside my single cab truck—it was going to be a tight squeeze.

Penelope squealed and squawked as soon as she heard Albert's voice, raising up on her little hooves to look out the window. I shook my head at the absurdity of it all but couldn't stop the grin that spread on my face.

After the joyful reunion between Albert and Penelope, Salem slinked over to the passenger side of the truck to rub against Albert's leg. My mouth dropped in disbelief—did that She-Demon really like everyone *but* me?

The aroma of flowers filled the truck, and I had to keep shoving them out of the way to see the road, my eyes swelling rapidly before the sneezing started. I rolled down my window hoping that would help, but the wind just pushed the flowers around chaotically, slapping me in the face twice.

It was with grim delight that I pulled into Albert's driveway. Not that I didn't enjoy Penelope, but now I could unload at least one animal. It had to be easier to just deal with one, right?

Albert led our merry pack of misfits to the front door, Salem refusing to stay in the truck. My spidey senses sent off an urgent alarm, though, and I grabbed Albert's arm as a sudden tingle ran from my skull down my spine.

"Wait. Something's not right." I examined the door—fresh scratch marks marred the gold surface, almost too faint to notice. I ordered Albert back to the truck, but he refused, his eyes stubborn as he shook his head, tightening his hold on Penelope. Looking heavenward, I briefly wondered what I'd done in this lifetime to deserve this.

I dropped the load of flowers I'd carried and used my T-shirt to turn the doorknob slowly. Nothing jumped out at us, so we proceeded inside, our steps quiet and deliberate. When I looked behind me I saw Albert's face, no trace of the jovial man he'd been in the truck. Replaced by the jovial, easygoing man, Albert now stood at full attention, eyes focused in front of us as we made our way through the house.

Looking around, I noticed signs someone had gone through his things. Subtle, but obvious. On the surface, everything looked undisturbed, but cupboard doors lay just barely open, items on the counters and curios moved fractionally, as evidenced by the dust patterns.

When we got to Albert's office, he rushed inside to where the safe stood. Dents and scratches were all the proof I needed to pull out my phone and call it in. Albert's eyes widened as he looked around, assessing the space.

Before I could stop him, he darted over to the bookcase, spry for the beating he'd taken only two nights ago. Reaching up, he pulled a worn paperback book off the shelf. I watched as he carefully flipped the pages, then pulled out a small USB key while sighing in relief.

Curious, I asked, "What's on it?"

"Proof," he replied with grim satisfaction.

Chapter Thirty Seven

SUMMER

AFTER THE EVENTS OF last night, not only was I demoralized, I also jumped at every noise and shadow. I couldn't believe how stupid I'd been, I knew better.

I'd completely forgotten about my car, but when I looked out the front window to the parking lot, there it sat. Someone had even tried to fix the dent. I looked closer. Yep. Someone had detailed it as well. My phone buzzed. I read the text from the unlisted number.

Keys are under the rear driver's side tire.

Sure enough, a key had been shoved under the tire, the sun glinting on the small edge sticking out. I tapped out a quick thank you text to Mr. Sam, shaking my head at the weird chain of events that had led to a Yakuza boss watching out for me. I had a feeling I had Auntie Miriam to thank for most of it.

I blew out a big sigh before tapping out a text:

Auntie, I need some help. I really messed up. Can we meet at WCC?

My phone vibrated, and I looked down to see Auntie Miriam's name flash across the screen.

"Hello?" I said, hoping my voice didn't tremble.

"Girl. You know my eyes don't like to read the texts. Call next time. Yes, I'll be there. What time you want to meet?"

"I'm heading in to work right now. Can we meet after my shift, around four?"

"I'll see you there. And, Summer," her voice softened, "be careful. There are rumblings of some Kahi'ino things happening."

My stomach clenched at her words. I know Auntie kept a close ear to the ground; if she was warning me, there was a reason.

"I will, Auntie," I promised.

Luckily, my shift passed uneventfully, nothing more serious than a few tourists with some minor cuts and scrapes from the lava rock and coral. I looked up toward Napua often. My heart hurt, I missed Lani so much and fear for her safety colored all of my thoughts. Lani was a tough girl, I knew she could handle herself, but what if they somehow found her on the mainland, far from where I could help? No one would ever know.

Just as my thoughts started racing to worst-case scenarios, I felt a buzz on my hip.

Girl, I'm fine. Quit worrying. You're going to get wrinkles!

Suspicious, I lifted my head and looked around. How on Earth had Lani known I was worrying about her right at that very moment? That was some witchy shit, if you asked me. Even though the number was unlisted, I knew it was her—she teased me all the time about getting 'worry' wrinkles.

The text made me smile though, and I felt some weight drop off my shoulders. Brody and I rushed to close up for the day. I didn't want to be late meeting Auntie Miriam, and Brody had a date that he called "Ono Wahine, and the mother of my future keiki." I just shook my head at his nonsense.

I straightened up the inside of the shack and stashed our rescue tubes behind our seats. "You know, one of these days you're going to have daughters of your own," I admonished.

Brody's trademark grin dimmed momentarily before he widened his smile, his perfect, straight white teeth blinding me. "Nope. Only boys in my family."

I rolled my eyes. "Okay, Gaston. Good luck with that."

He smirked at me and then walked me to my car. He teased me about Cole along the way, but I noticed an uncharacteristic tension in him. When I glanced over, I noticed him surveilling the parking lot. I pursed my lips at him, and his cheesy grin faded, replaced by embarrassment at being caught.

As I was getting into my car, I leaned over and kissed his cheek. "Thank you," I said, my voice soft. Brody blushed and shuffled his feet before waving away my thanks.

"I don't know what you're talking about," he said, before heading over to his white Tacoma parked two spots over. We waved and I headed to Waimea to meet Auntie.

Auntie Miriam sat at one of the picnic tables in the central courtyard, two glasses of reddish pink liquid on the table in front of her. She gestured for me to sit, and I took the spot across from her, glad for the sun as the wind began to blow. Everyone thinks Hawaii is a warm tropical place, but Mauna Kea regularly gets snow in the winter, and Waimea's climate was notorious for its moody weather. One day warm and sunny, the next, cold and rainy.

Fizzy, cold bubbles tickled my nose as I sniffed at the drink in front of me. I raised an eyebrow at Miriam.

"Hibiscus soda," she answered my unspoken question. The first sip soothed my throat, the sweet, flowery flavor interesting and understated. I set the glass down, uncertainty swamping me now that Auntie sat looking at me, an indecipherable look on her face. I swallowed and rubbed my eyes, sending up a silent prayer before looking her in the eye.

"I screwed up," I told her, shame washing over me at her disapproving look as I told her about last night.

She said nothing for long moments after I finished, and anxiety breathed fire through me. Her first question surprised me, though.

"What did you do with the pendant?" her tone was filled with mild curiosity, as her hand twirled her bracelet repeatedly, her gaze focused away from me.

I hesitated before answering, something about her demeanor triggered a red flag warning in my head. Cataloguing all I knew about Miriam: hell raiser in her youth, similar to Lani, breaker of male hearts in several continents and countries, connected to the Hawaiian underground, had walked a very fine, gray line with the law in her younger years, member of The Nation of Hawai'i.

Ahh- that was it. The Nation of Hawaii had been fighting for sovereignty from the United States and had a very keen interest in returning the island and its inhabitants back to Hawaiian governance. Known for quietly reclaiming Hawaiian artifacts, important documents, etc., I'm sure they were very interested in the Lei o mano and pendant, especially if the story Cole told me that the holder of both had infinite power was true, despite his skepticism.

Auntie Miriam read my face and reached across the table and squeezed my hand gently. "That pendant means a great deal to my people. We'd like to honor it by placing it in the museum in perpetuity."

Her words were like a punch to the gut. This whole time, I'd only been thinking about Lani. I hadn't even considered how much this drama might affect other Hawaiian people. I dropped my head in shame.

"I gave it to Cole," I said, my voice muffled.

Based on her sharp intake of breath, I guessed that was the exact wrong answer. How had everything gone so completely, horribly wrong?

"Call him. I need to speak with him before he does something stupid, like enter it into evidence in the case." Urgency colored her voice.

Immediately, I grabbed my phone and dialed. "Hello?" The deep rasp of his voice had my insides jumping to attention.

"Cole. It's me and Auntie Miriam. Have you done anything with the pendant yet?"

Silence rang for a moment before he answered. "No, not yet. Why?" There was something in his tone I couldn't quite read.

Auntie Miriam took over. "You need to bring it to us right now. I'll explain everything when you get here. Don't disappoint me young man." She hit the red button to end the call, and my eyes got big as I looked up at her.

She shrugged. "I'm not willing to debate. He'll do the right thing," she said to herself almost as much as to me.

Chapter Thirty Eight

COLE

I STARED AT THE phone in my hand for a moment, in disbelief that I had been commanded and dismissed by a five-foot two auntie so casually.

Albert cleared his throat next to me, where we sat poring over the records he'd saved on all the auctions and bids placed on items. I turned my head towards him, "Auntie Miriam," I said.

He recoiled, a look of fear on his face. "I think my balls just shriveled," he replied. I laughed for the first time all day. After calling in the burglary at Albert's house I'd stayed to help him deal with the aftermath and sift through the evidence he'd been compiling over the years. Insurance is what he called it. He showed me the pouch he kept on him at all times. "Normally I carry the USB with my files on me, but my pants were a little snug, so I hid it here." He pointed to the hollowed-out book he'd snagged earlier.

Albert was an enigma. When I first met him, he seemed a bit like a polished peacock. That image didn't align with the ruthless world he'd involved himself in, or with the underground auctions he facilitated. His cleverness in the handling of all of this information showed someone with a high level of intelligence and strategic thinking. Curiosity snaked through me, but I ruthlessly tamped it down in order to find something, *anything*, that could help me close this case and keep Summer safe.

So far, what I'd read lined up with Jonah's notes. Underground auction, uber wealthy players, a much-coveted artifact for sale to the highest bidder, and, other than Wainright, the players all had reputations and ties with dangerous organizations.

I'd slogged through dozens of documents, my eyes burning from staring at the screen for so long. Auntie Miriam's call was a welcome distraction from screen time, but I couldn't help but wonder what stake she had in the pendant. My first instinct was to call back and interrogate her about her reasons, but, well, she terrified me. I agreed with Albert's sentiment.

Penelope and Salem were playing a game of chase, and when I stood up, Salem parkoured off of my leg, digging her claws into skin as she did so. I squealed and so did Penelope, but for different reasons. Penelope looked like she was having the time of her life, her little tail twirling so fast it looked almost like the rotors of a helicopter in the air. My eyes followed Salem, and I swear she threw a self-satisfied smirk back at me as I rubbed the spot she'd clawed.

I grabbed a load of papers, documents Albert printed out for me, then looked for Salem's crate.

Albert watched me and said, "Leave her. Penelope hasn't had this much fun in ages."

Relief to be rid of that She-Demon, at least for the day, swept over me. With a sigh of happiness, I headed out the door, whistling. Then I remembered something Summer had told me the other day—she said only creepers and serial killers whistled. I halted my forward momentum and stopped whistling before continuing out to my truck. Not that I agreed with her about whistling being the territory of creepy serial killers, but I didn't want her to think that about me.

I rummaged around in my truck for the pendant, thankful when my hand grasped the black box under my seat. I peeked inside where the pendant lay nestled. Honestly, to me, it looked a lot like the pendants sold at the ABC store for ten bucks to tourists. I shrugged my shoulders and fired up my motor, pointing my truck uphill toward our meeting spot.

Auntie Miriam and Summer sat outside at a picnic table in front of the cluster of stores that made up the Waimea Shopping Center, colorful chickens surrounding them in the hopes of a few crumbs.

I'd never understood the phrase 'gird my loins' until I walked up to the table, two sets of speculative eyes on me.

Auntie Miriam's lively brown eyes ran up and down the length of me before landing back on my face. I understood how she earned her reputation as a heartbreaker—her come-hither smile and assessing eyes were likely to draw in any man with a pulse. I shook my head. *What was I thinking?*

"My, my. You've grown into quite the man, Cole Peterson," she said, a hint of smoke and invitation in her voice.

"Knock it off, Auntie," Summer said, irritation pouring off of her. *Wait- was she jealous?* I grinned at the thought, then sobered when she gave me stink eye.

Miriam patted the spot next to her on the bench and I slid in, careful not to get too close. A breeze from Mauna Kea drifted over me, bringing the scent of Miriam's perfume, a combination of vanilla and something else.

"So, Cole. Summer tells me you are holding on to the pendant for safekeeping."

I nodded in the affirmative and she continued. "I'd like to request that you allow me to safeguard it with my people, where it belongs anyway. Given the nature of the legend attached to it, I feel the pendant could be dangerous in the hands of anyone not respectful of its true meaning."

My eyes traveled across the table to Summer, who watched me closely for an answer. Normally, there were proper channels required for any sort of evidence gained in the investigation of a murder, or any crime for that matter. While I understood Miriam's desire to have the pendant returned to her people, I knew that in order to build a solid case against Demyan, the pendant would be a key component used in the evidence against him.

The problem lay in the way the pendant was obtained. In order to admit it into evidence, I would have to report where and how I came into possession of it, which would put Summer not only in legal trouble but also most likely in danger from Demyan.

Auntie Miriam pulled her trump card, easily reading the cascade of thoughts on my face to turn the screws and get me to capitulate.

"Summer could go to jail if HPD finds out how you got the pendant."

Summer choked on her drink, a horrified look on her face.

She continued. "But more importantly, if Demyan were to find out what happened, her life could be in danger. I know that's a risk none of us is willing to take." She gazed fondly at Summer and Summer rolled her eyes, earning her a kick under the table from Miriam.

Miriam was good, I had to hand it to her. I could see now why she was the unspoken boss of this island. I wasn't going to give up without a fight though.

The question was—how was I going to gain control of this case? I'd already started mentally counting in my head all the ways I'd already broken protocol, while also wondering what angle Miriam was working and if she'd honor her word.

"If, and I mean if, I hand it over to you, for now anyway, I will need your ho'ohiki that if the pendant becomes the key avenue to prove Demyan's guilt, you immediately return it to me, no questions asked." My voice might have juddered just a bit on the last part, but I firmed my jaw and looked Miriam squarely in the eye as I delivered my ultimatum.

She squinted at me, and I got the distinct sense she was looking for any weakness she could exploit. Seeing none, she gritted her teeth and held out her hand. "Deal."

Chapter Thirty Nine

SUMMER

WHILE WE WAITED FOR Cole, I subtly tried to gather intel on Auntie Miriam's relationship status with Mr. Sam. I watched her face soften, a giddy smile playing on her lips when she received a text from him. I'd known Auntie since I was ten years old, my mom and Miriam having known each other for years. My mom once confided in me that Auntie Miriam carried the weight of her lineage, and felt especially responsible for ushering in a new generation of Hawaiians to be raised with a love and reverence for the aina, as well as each other. Over the years I'd witnessed first hand her ability to dole out tough love along with a warm shoulder.

In fact, the whole reason Lani and I even became friends was because of Auntie Miriam. I remember going to the beach with my mom, her excitement about getting together with Miriam only slightly irritating. I'd rolled my eyes when she told me Miriam was bringing her niece Lani, who was ten years old, just like me. My mom was always trying to get me to be more social and make friends, when I'd rather be swimming in the ocean or reading a book than talking to people.

When Lani and I first set eyes on each other, it was hate at first sight. I hated her perfectly petite figure, and beautifully curly dark shiny hair, framed around a delicate, heart-shaped face. Her liquid brown eyes stared at me with contempt.

I heard her mutter, "Useless haole." Miriam also heard and cuffed her on the back of her head. My only recourse was to ignore her, and if I couldn't do that, be better than her. When an extensive set of colossal waves rolled in, I decided to show off and headed into the foamy surf before diving cleanly underneath the next wave, my snorkel mask clutched in my hand.

I swam out much farther than I normally did and was surprised when Lani surfaced next to me only seconds later. I stared at her in astonishment; I'd never met anyone who could keep up with me in the water. Just behind her, I saw a dark shape floating in the water. My eyes got big until I recognized the oblong shell of a green turtle.

Lani noticed it too, and we both cautiously swam a little closer to look at it. We noticed a plastic net normally used to hold oranges wrapped around the turtle's head. Without conscious thought or coordination, we both swam calmly to the turtle so as not to scare it and worked together to untangle it. Once freed, the turtle dipped underwater, but then resurfaced and nudged us both gently, as if to say thank you.

That moment cemented us as best friends. Every time my family visited the Big Island, Lani and I were glued at the hip. When I finally made the permanent move, Elliot became part of our group, our duo becoming a trio.

I sighed now as I thought of Lani. Auntie Miriam's head snapped up and she scrutinized my face. "Lani's going to be okay. That girl is like a goddamned tardigrade. Nothing's going to take her out." I nodded and smiled, just to appease her, but was also a little impressed she knew what a tardigrade was.

"Now look, have I ever been wrong about anything?" she asked me. I lifted a finger and started to remind her about the time she was convinced the Chinese were spying on her using specially trained myna birds, but hastily put it down when she cocked an eyebrow at me in challenge.

Luckily, Cole pulled up just then, and we both watched as he made his way to our table. From the corner of my eye, I saw Miriam lower her sunglasses and give him a thorough appraisal.

"Auntie!" I said, scandalized.

"I'm human too," she said before turning back to survey him closer. I shook my head at her in consternation.

Throughout the conversation with Cole, I watched as Miriam played him like a Stradivarius, softly at first, warming him up before manipulating him into handing over the pendant. The only surprise to me was the fact that Cole pushed back and got Auntie to agree to his terms. She didn't like it, but somewhere deep down inside she must've recognized the logic in his words.

Before leaving, I hugged Auntie, whispering in her ear, "You need to teach me someday."

Her cackle of laughter had me smiling for the first time all day. "I don't know if you're ready yet, grasshopper." She kissed my cheek, then hopped into her Cadillac, tooting her horn as she drove out of the parking lot.

Cole, quiet while he watched our interplay just lifted an eyebrow at me. I waved my hand at him. "Girl stuff."

He nodded and then asked if I had any plans for the rest of the evening, hesitation winding through his voice.

I slung my arm over his shoulder and leaned in. "After watching a master at work, I'm pretty thirsty. Wanna buy me a drink?"

He bristled a little before deflating. "She really is a master, isn't she?" His tone was almost admiring. "Where do you want to go?"

We agreed to meet at the Seafood Bar in Kawaihae. On the drive back down the hill, I thought about Cole. What his motivations were, how he must be feeling, and the type of pressure he must be under. I couldn't help but feel sorry, and if I were being honest, responsible for the shitstorm he was now part of.

While driving down, Elliot called and I invited him to join us. He declined, saying he didn't want to be a third wheel on our date.

"It's not a date," I insisted. "We're just meeting for a drink, then heading home for dinner. You don't mind if Cole comes to dinner, do you? I can uninvite him if it's a problem." Worry twisted my gut—I didn't want Elliot to feel left out.

Silence. *Shit.*

"What? Sorry, I dropped my phone," Elliot said.

I repeated my question.

"No, as much as I never thought I'd get along with the "Man", it's nice to have an officer around."

I blew out the breath I'd been holding and my stomach relaxed. I turned into the parking lot and promised Elliot I'd text when we were on our way home.

Cole hopped out of his truck, and I couldn't help but admire the way his jeans outlined his very fine ass. Mesmerized, I almost missed the grim look on his face as I parked and watched him walk over to my car.

"What's wrong?" I asked, worry rising instantly.

He held out his phone and I read the text on his screen, then searched his face. "What does this mean?"

His jaw hardened, and as I watched, he transformed into cop mode. "It means the HPD has probable cause to search Demyan's boat."

Chapter Forty

COLE

I WATCHED AS SUMMER's face went through a variety of emotions, hope being the most predominant.

"So, the cloth you found on Demyan's boat has Wainright's DNA?"

I nodded. "Not only his DNA, but the fibers match the shirt he was wearing when you pulled his body out of the water."

"Okay, this is good, right?" she asked. "This keeps the pendant out of the investigation."

Before I could answer, my phone rang. *Kregness.* I held up my finger and walked a short distance away.

"Hey, what'd you find out?" I asked him.

"Chief wants to do this one by the book, wrap everything up with a neat little bow. He's already talking about how much press he'll get." I could almost hear Kregness shaking his head in disgust. "Legal went to the judge to get warrants, but because Demyan's a foreigner, there's more red tape to sort through. I'll let you know, but my guess is we won't get warrants any sooner than tomorrow."

I struggled to tamp down my impatience. While I understood the need to follow protocol to the letter on this, worry for Summer ate at me. I hung up, then called Jack Hall.

After I filled him in on the latest news, I asked if he'd heard anything from the Chief yet. He snorted. "Nah. I don't think he likes me too much. Rumor has it he's hoping to close a high-profile investigation and get reinstated in Honolulu."

Good riddance. Chief was walking the line in a lot of ways, and I didn't trust him. The sooner he went back to Oahu, the sooner he was out of my hair.

"Demyan's going to lawyer up the second we get close, you know that, right?"

Frustration wound through me as I pictured Demyan walking free. "Yeah, I figured," I replied.

"Honestly, Cole, the only way I think we can prosecute is if we can get him to confess. Otherwise, his high-priced lawyers will keep things tied up in court for years while he walks around free."

I knew Jack was right, but I didn't see a confession happening. "Anyway, buddy, I'll be there whenever, just let me know," Jack said before hanging up.

Summer surveyed my face before touching my cheek gently. My frustration level went down, and I smiled at her, although the smile felt more like a grimace.

"Hey, why don't we skip drinks and just head back to my place for dinner?" Summer suggested.

Relieved, I agreed. I didn't think I had it in me to socialize with anyone else right now. I briefly squeezed her hand before getting back in my truck.

As I followed her back to Waikoloa, my thoughts turned back to the investigation. The cloth I'd found was damning, but his lawyers would eat holes in the evidence. They'd argue anyone could've placed the cloth there, and even with the paperwork Albert had provided that showed probable cause, the evidence was thin at best.

Outrage welled up at the idea he'd go free. Before I had too much time to get worked up about it, I received a photo from Albert—Penelope and Salem were snuggled together in Penelope's bed, fast asleep.

You can leave Salem here tonight—I think Penelope's in love.

I shook my head, but couldn't help but smile, my liberation from the She-Beast in sight.

As I pulled up to Summer and Elliot's condo, I wondered how much the condos in the complex were selling for. My apartment in Kona was fine, but lately I'd been looking at real estate and thinking about buying instead of renting. My landlord had texted me earlier today that a water line had burst and I'd need to find somewhere to stay tonight and maybe tomorrow. My mom answered *yes* immediately when I'd sent her a text explaining the situation and asking if I could bunk with her for the night. It wasn't a big deal, but those kinds of things kept happening at our complex.

In the parking lot, Summer stood next to her car, pinned in by the old lady who had visited to complain about my parking last week. Even from where I stood, I could hear Summer getting bawled out.

"Listen, Karen, I hear what you're saying. But we've had a crisis going on and my friend has been spending a lot of time here to help, okay?"

The old lady squawked. "I told you—my name's not Karen!" She balled up her fists at her side, self-righteous anger radiating off of her. "There are only two spots per condo. You've taken up three spots every night for the last week. This is unacceptable. Management has already been contacted. You'll be getting a letter!" And with that, the old lady shook her fist at Summer and stalked off. Summer looked at me and rolled her eyes.

"I don't want to get you in trouble with the condo association," I told her.

She waved away my comment. "No worries, Karen–not–Karen is a notorious parking lot snitch. The condo board is pretty lenient about parking, especially when there are so many open spots."

We both glanced around at the half full lot. "If you're sure," I said.

Summer nodded and then snagged my hand, leading me into the condo. It felt nice, that normal gesture.

Elliot stood in the kitchen, stirring something in a pot, the heavenly sent of curry wafting in the air. He waved and I waved back, then Summer filled him in on the parking lot fiasco.

Elliot snorted. "One of these days, Karen's going to push the wrong buttons of the wrong person."

We sat on the lanai and ate dinner, watching the last rays of the sun go down. Peace washed through me. Wainright's murder investigation loomed large, but for just a moment it felt nice to relax and enjoy Summer and Elliot's company.

They must've felt the same way. Their faces became animated as they argued about who the best James Bond was, their conversation light and easy.

"Daniel Craig," I said, inserting myself into the conversation.

"Exactly!" Elliot crowed at Summer. Summer pouted, then stuck her tongue out at us. Laughter bubbled up.

A knock at the door interrupted the moment, and I followed Elliot as he went to answer the door. He peeked through the peephole and then shrugged his shoulders. "No one's there," he said.

I heard a ticking noise as he opened the door, slamming it and throwing him to the ground just as the door exploded into pieces all around us.

Chapter Forty One
SUMMER

Smoke filled the room, my ears ringing as I watched splinters of wood fly down the hallway. The front door lay partially blown off its hinges, uneven patches of wood remaining in the frame, like jagged shark teeth.

Horror washed over me, and I raced over to where Elliot and Cole lay, Cole covering Elliot's body, the back of his head covered in wooden shards, spots of blood welling up in places. Frantically, I clawed the broken door out of the way and brushed the debris off of Cole. I rolled him off of Elliot as gently as I could, his body limp, eyes closed.

Tears pricked my eyes as I leaned over and looked into his face, stroking his cheek and begging him to wake up. Elliot shifted and curled into a ball, still for a minute before popping his eyes open and sitting up abruptly. His eyes shifted to Cole and we both called his name, shaking him gently.

A small grin appeared on his face and one eye cracked open. "Am I in heaven?" he asked. The relief that washed over me was overwhelming and I bent down closer and kissed him softly. Strong arms wrapped around me and held me in place. Cole deepened the kiss, and I willingly went along with it until I heard Elliot clear his throat.

"I hate to break up this romantic moment, but I'd like to point out that a bomb just went off at our front door. Maybe we need to focus on a few other things right now, yeah?"

Reluctantly, I shifted, and Cole's arms tightened for a moment before letting me go. He sat up in stages, slow and steady as I helped him, before he gained his balance and looked around. First at Elliot and me, then at the broken door, laying mostly in pieces all around him.

A siren wailed in the distance. Now that I knew Cole and Elliot were okay, my whole body shook, my teeth chattering so hard I worried I might crack one. Elliot moved first, helping me over to the couch and wrapping a comforting arm around my shoulder. Cole made his way painstakingly over to us, movements jerky and sluggish. He sat on the other side of me and wrapped his arm around my waist, which is how the police found us.

HPD finally left after more than an hour, warning us to be careful and find somewhere else to stay until they found the perpetrator. They wanted to take Cole to the hospital to get checked out, but Cole adamantly refused. My brain was so muddled I couldn't even think through the next steps, robotically packing an overnight bag, throwing clothes in randomly. A text came through from Mr. Sam.

I heard about the bomb. My yacht is moored off the Mauna Kea coast, a car will be there in 15 minutes. Please consider yourself and your friends my honored guests.

I showed the text to Elliot and Cole. Their reactions were opposite of each other. Elliot said, "Ooooohhhh!" and clapped his hands together in excitement. Cole's posture stiffened and he hardened his jaw. I sensed he was going to decline when my phone buzzed again. *Auntie Miriam.*

Tell the cop I give my word you'll all be safe. And for God's sake stop finding trouble!

Cole's lips twitched when he read the text, and he agreed with as much grace as possible, nodding once and muttering, "Okay."

I'm sure the idea of sleeping on a Yakuza boss's yacht didn't align with his cop values, but at this time of night it was probably the best option we could get. Minutes later, a black Escalade pulled up by the front door and Mr. Sam's men hopped out and opened the car door for us.

As we climbed in, I hoped I wasn't making a huge mistake, but knowing Auntie Miriam vouched for Mr. Sam went a long way in diffusing my anxiety.

The same couldn't be said of Cole. He sat on the edge of the seat, one hand on the handle, eyes scanning back and forth between the two men up front. Elliot, on the other hand, chattered nonstop and even bounced in the seat a little. I watched as he ran his hand down the leather seats before saying, "It must be easier to get blood out of leather seats than cloth, huh?"

We all froze, except for Elliot, oblivious as he leaned forward, waiting for an answer. The man in the passenger seat broke the silence. "It is much easier. Better to keep bodies in the back though, boss doesn't like blood on his seats."

The driver growled at his buddy and smacked him on the back of the head. "What my coworker means to say is that we don't like *any* of our passengers to bleed, so we take the utmost care to prevent that."

I shuddered, and if possible, Cole puckered up even more, his hands white from the grip on the door handle.

Elliot nodded sagely, as if this were an everyday conversation for him. I looked heavenward, wondering how on Earth we'd ended up in this predicament.

Before I could spend any time thinking about it, we pulled up to the harbor where a boat tender was waiting at the dock for us, two large men manning it. Our driver gestured elegantly toward the boat, and we all hopped out of the car and climbed onboard.

The ride out to the yacht, a looming white monolith of sleek, graceful proportions, went by quickly. The salty ocean air soothed my nervous system somewhat, and by the time we slid up next to the yacht some of the tension in my neck had eased.

Elliot sat up at the stern, holding on as the wind blew his hair back, looking for all the world like a carefree titan of industry, enjoying the spoils of his work. I had to shake my head, even as a small smile formed. At least Elliot embraced each moment with abandon, a feat I still had yet to master.

Once onboard the giant yacht, we were shown to our rooms, tastefully decorated in Japanese-style simplicity. Knowing Elliot and Cole were on either side of me went a long way in soothing my frayed nerves. The events of the day caught up with me, and even as I sent a longing look towards the giant soaking tub in the corner of the room, I crashed on the softest, most comfortable bed I'd ever slept in fully clothed, asleep the second my head hit the pillow.

When I finally woke up, the sun was high in the sky and I groaned, realizing I'd missed the start of my lifeguard shift. I shifted closer to the sleek mahogany nightstand and grabbed my phone to text Brody.

There were ten missed messages from him. Ugh. Just as I pulled up his number to call him back, a new text came in.

Auntie called to let me know you wouldn't be in today. Don't worry sis, I got you covered. Hope you feel better soon.

While I wasn't sure what Miriam told him, I figured I'd play along for now. My stomach growled, reminding me I'd slept through breakfast. I opened the door to go in search of some food.

And ran right into Cole's rock-hard chest, his powerful arms snaking up to stop me from falling.

I looked up into his beautiful turquoise blue eyes, green flecks scattered within, and tipped my head up, lips puckered for a kiss. He shook his head. "No time for that. We've got a problem."

Chapter Forty Two
COLE

"Only one?" she replied.

I stared at Summer for a second. Then I laughed. Despite everything happening right now, I laughed. A full bellied, deep from within laugh. This crazy, frustrating, beautiful woman delighted me. There was no other word. As I looked at her now, her brow puckered in confusion, I bent down and kissed her.

Just when things were getting interesting, Elliot's door opened, and he popped his head out. "What's going on?"

Summer growled quietly, and a dumb smile spilled across my face. I vowed when this was over, Summer and I were going to go on a proper date, with flowers, dinner, candles, and alone time.

Summer gripped my arm, snagging my attention. "You said we have a problem—what is it?"

Her question brought me crashing back to reality. I watched her face as I delivered the news. "Demyan's disappeared."

Elliot broke in. "Disappeared? What does that mean?"

"HPD went to serve a warrant at the Fairmont, but he was already gone. Everyone cleared out around three am according to staff. HPD is watching the airports and harbors, but so far nothing. Just poof! Gone."

"So that means he could be anywhere," Summer said. I watched the expression on Summer's face—fear tinged with something I couldn't define.

I nodded. "Interpol is involved, and I think with all the heat on him he's gone to ground."

I noticed a strange, unholy glint in her eye as she processed the information, and I glanced at Elliot to see what his reaction was. He also watched Summer; trepidation on his face.

"Whatever you're plotting, just stop it right now. Demyan is dangerous. We almost got blown up last night. Let the authorities handle this," I ordered.

Summer just nodded distractedly before asking Elliot, "Do you know where we can get any food up in this joint?"

Far from reassured, I let it go for now, but vowed to keep an eye on her and make sure she didn't do anything stupid.

Elliot flung open his door with a flourish, gesturing like Vanna White at a lavish spread on the table in his room. There was a basket filled with every kind of pastry you could imagine, small jars of jams and jellies artistically nestled inside. A covered silver serving platter sat next to the basket, the scent of bacon making my mouth water. Various platters blanketed the table, crystal pitchers full of different varieties of juice sat on a side table nearby.

As one, we fell on the food like rabid animals, not talking except for grunts and gestures at specific platters. When my stomach ached from the amount of food I'd stuffed in it, I sat back and surveyed the destruction. We'd put a major dent in the food, but there was still an enormous amount left.

I looked over at Summer and smiled as she took an enormous bite of the strawberry lilikoi scone in her hand, her cheeks puffing out as she tried to keep it all in her mouth and chew. There was something about a woman who *liked* food and wasn't afraid to eat in front of me that warmed my heart.

I sipped my coffee and thought about our predicament. If Demyan was in the wind, that meant he could be any-where. A smart man would cut bait and run, but I suspect-ed Demyan's ego had been bruised enough that he wanted revenge.

A knock at the door interrupted my musings. Auntie Miriam walked in, holding hands with Mr. Sam. Miriam glanced with amusement at the table and then shared a very intimate look with Mr. Sam that had me shifting uncom-fortably.

He smiled at her, a look of tender fondness on his face before he turned and addressed us. "I hope your stay was comfortable?"

Elliot nodded and bowed. Summer snorted at him, earning her an evil glare. He straightened up self-con-sciously and then approached Mr. Sam, eyes lowered, shoul-ders hunched slightly. Holding out his hand he introduced himself.

Mr. Sam nodded his head, a barely perceptible acknowl-edgement of Elliot and Elliot bowed again, earning another snort from Summer, Miriam, and myself. While he wasn't brave enough to glare at Miriam, Summer and I were both on the receiving end of some serious stink eye.

Mr. Sam noted the interactions, his eyes twinkling and lips quirking up into an amused smile. "May we impose on your morning? I have some news you will be interested in."

Summer straightened in her seat abruptly, her fingers tapping out a rhythm on the table. Elliot watched Summer's reaction with wide eyes and slowly nodded his head at Mr. Sam.

Mr. Sam turned toward me, eyebrows lifted in question. I cleared my throat, still ambivalent about interacting with a known Yakuza boss and stalling for time.

Mr. Sam just waited patiently, his posture relaxed and open. Eventually I capitulated, albeit reluctantly, and nodded sharply at him. His smile widened at my obvious discomfort, but gracious in his victory, he stated, "I think you'll want to hear this Detective Peterson."

He let go of Miriam's hand, albeit with obvious reluctance, sending her an affectionate look. Dimples appeared as she looked at Mr. Sam from under her eyelashes coquettishly. A soft look crossed his face before he turned back to us.

"As Detective Peterson has likely already told you, Demyan has vanished. My sources say he's been spotted on the island. I have pulled all of my men from their current assignments, and we are now focused on rooting him out from whatever cave he may be hiding in." He paced around the room, stopping to gaze at an ancient jade and gold vase sitting inside the recessed wall shelf, the muted light within the wall reflecting off the gold accents. He seemed to ponder his next words before he continued.

"My team is feeding the HPD information on any potential hiding spots. As soon as we have confirmation, HPD will be notified. But," he turned to look at us, "you have targets on your backs until he is located. I'd like you to consider yourselves my most welcome and honored guests until then."

I looked to see what Summer's reaction was, but she was typing furiously into her phone, her fingers a blur. The room got quiet, all eyes on Summer. It took her a moment to notice. Her head whipped up and her gaze traveled over our faces. "What?" she said, her tone defensive.

"I think Mr. Sam is worried you're going to do something stupid and wants you to stay put," Elliot said, as if Summer were a slow, dense child. I saw her kick him under the table, causing the table to bounce as his knee hit the underside. He reached over to pinch her, murder in his eyes, when Miriam intervened, cuffing them both on the back of the head. Elliot looked properly chastised, however, Summer's face puckered up, her eyes tight with defiance.

Mr. Sam took in the scene, his face and eyes appearing relaxed. His only tell was the slight tap of his foot. "You have free rein here on the *Nama Maru*. My staff is here to assist you. Please don't hesitate to ask for whatever you need."

Summer jumped out of her seat. "I need to go home and pick up a few things."

"I assure you, my men will be happy to fetch whatever you might need."

She shook her head back and forth, a mutinous expression plain on her face. "No. I need to go. Respectfully, as much as I appreciate your generosity," she swung her arms wide to encompass the table, remnants of breakfast still spread about, "you can't keep me here against my will. I need to go get a few things and then I'll be happy to come right back."

"The boat tender is at your disposal," he conceded. "But, I would ask that you allow my men to accompany you if you leave the *Nama Maru*."

Summer's mouth opened as if she might argue, but Mr. Sam's next words stopped her. "Your friends have already paid a heavy price for your interference."

Summer's gaze lowered and her arms wrapped around her torso as if to comfort herself.

"Please permit my men to watch over you." This time Summer nodded, gaze still on the ground.

Chapter Forty Three

SUMMER

Mr. Sam and Auntie Miriam left, but not before Auntie threw a suspicious look my way, wagging her finger at me in warning. A shiver ran through me—that woman could freeze a person in their tracks with just one lifted brow.

Guilt flooded through me at Mr. Sam's words. He was right. Because I'd messed up, Elliot and Cole were almost killed. If I hadn't accidentally taken the pendant, Demyan never would have come after me. The only thing I could figure was he must have hacked the resort's surveillance footage after he realized the pendant was gone and caught Cole and I coming out of his room.

I looked over at them now. My boys. Elliot, his glasses smudged and hair sticking up at all angles, his usually well-coiffed look nowhere to be found. And Cole, still wearing the same clothes as yesterday, smudges of black soot dotting his T-shirt, watching me closely.

I held my hands up. "All I want to do is pick up a change of clothes and some toiletries and I'll come right back. Promise. Mr. Sam has everything under control and I'm just going to wait it out."

Elliot looked suspicious. "Mmhmm. Then who were you texting when you should've been listening to Mr. Sam? Who, by the way, gives total Pat Morita vibes."

"None of your business," I replied, but I watched Cole's face as I answered. Worry lines were etched across his forehead, deep valleys between his eyebrows. And disappointment. *Shit.* My idea to handle this myself and leave them out of it disappeared in a poof of disapproval from Elliot and disappointment from Cole.

I blew out a long sigh and motioned Cole and Elliot over to show them my phone. A picture of Penelope popped up on the screen, her little hooves tied together, and a note pinned to her collar:

Bring me the pendant before we make bacon. Come alone, tell no one.

The address of a deserted lot near the harbor was scrawled on the note along with a time—11:00am. The hands of the miniature koa wood grandfather clock in the corner of the cabin read 10:07.

"They have Penelope." I said, my voice quiet.

Elliot and Cole looked horrified.

"Wha—" just as Cole spoke his phone rang. Grimly, he lifted the screen so we could see. *Albert.*

"Cole, Penelope's gone! I need to put out an all-points bulletin or missing and endangered pig broadcast or something. I can't find her anywhere!" he wailed. In the background we heard growling and screeching and glasses breaking.

"Whoa, okay. Tell me what you know."

"I let Penelope and Salem out to go potty twenty minutes ago, when I heard a crash and Penelope squealing. I ran outside and Salem was the only one in the pen, hissing and spitting toward the road. I heard tires spinning on the gravel, but by the time I made it to the end of the driveway it was empty." Albert's words came in quick gasps as he tried to catch his breath. "I don't know what to do. You have to help me get her back!" More glass breaking and thumps in the background.

"Okay, of course I'll help. Albert's what's going on at your house? What are those noises?"

"That's Salem. She's been like this ever since Penelope got pig-napped. She went crazy—she's tearing the house apart!" Albert's pitch got higher and higher as he talked, his panic palpable through the phone.

"Alright, this is what we're going to do. I want you to load up Salem into her cat carrier and then meet us at Kawaihae Harbor in twenty minutes, okay? I need you to stay calm buddy. We'll get Penelope back." Cole ended the call and then looked at us grimly, a muscle in his cheek twitching.

"Guess we're going to Kawaihae," he said, his tone low and steely.

"No. You guys stay here. This is all my fault. If I hadn't inadvertently taken the pendant, none of this would have happened."

Elliot made a rude noise next to me and then lightly cuffed the back of my head. "We're the three musketeers. We stick together. Let's go save Penelope." His grin was lopsided as he looked between me and Cole.

Cole lifted my chin, forcing me to look him in the eye. "We go together," he ground out. He stalked over to the door and tossed it open. Elliot and I watched, our eyes big, as he grabbed his backpack, his broad shoulders making it look tiny, before he motioned for us to follow him.

Mr. Sam's staff had us on the tender and headed to shore within minutes. The only snag came when we got to the harbor and realized they intended to shadow us the entire time. The note said to come alone—we needed to lose these guys if we wanted to save Penelope.

Albert pulled up in a cloud of dust, gravel and dirt flying before he came to a screeching stop in front of us, not bothering to turn off his bright canary-yellow Mustang before hopping out, panic plainly written in the lines of his face.

He thrust the cat carrier at Elliot and latched on to Cole's arm. "Have you heard anything yet? Did the police find her?" The whites of his eyes showed and fear radiated off of him.

I rubbed his back as Cole spoke to him in a soothing voice, attempting to calm him down. "Not yet, Albert. We believe Demyan has Penelope and is holding her in exchange for the pendant we took from his safe."

Albert's eyes bounced back and forth between Cole and I before he let out a howling wail of anguish. I closed my eyes against the wash of guilt as I felt Albert's despair.

Taking a deep breath against the onslaught of emotion, I fought for calm, trying to formulate a plan that wouldn't end in me dying.

Chapter Forty Four

COLE

10:43AM. WE HAD SEVENTEEN minutes to get to the meeting site. Not enough time to scope out places to hide, and certainly not enough time to talk Summer out of whatever harebrained idea she had cooking. Even now as I looked at her, her eyes had a far-off look, some sort of scheme cooking.

"Okay, here's what we're going to do. Elliot, you and Albert wait here with Salem. Summer, you and I will head to the drop site and stall for time. Meanwhile, I'll pin HPD with our coordinates." I looked at the faces surrounding me, all of them scrunched up, heads shaking no, arms crossed, like some weird choreographed dance routine.

"No way are we staying behind while you run off and fight the bad guys," Elliot said.

Albert agreed. "Yeah, why should you get to have all the fun? Besides, I have a score to settle with them. You don't just break into a man's house and steal his pig." His finger jabbed in the air as he made his point.

My eyes traveled over to Summer, watching her face as she smiled, amused at Albert. The look on her face as she turned to me grew sober, however.

"I caused this. I need to fix it. Besides, the note said to come alone. If they see anyone else, they might hurt Penelope just to prove a point." Albert whimpered as he listened.

I wasn't giving up. "No. He'll definitely hurt you when he finds out you don't have the pendant. This isn't a game, Summer." My tone came out harsher than I intended, but worry for her consumed me.

She flinched at my words but stood strong, arguing her point. "It's precisely because I *don't* have the pendant that I'm safe. He needs me to get the pendant. He can't get the pendant if he kills me."

Elliot choked audibly at Summer's words, terror plainly written on his face.

"Guys, we're wasting time. It's a seven-minute drive and we have ten minutes until the deadline. I have to go!"

Summer shook off Elliot's hand and tried to turn away, but he grabbed her and spun her around. "Absolutely not. Either we all go, or no one goes."

Albert, who'd been silent through this exchange jumped in. "That's right. We're all going. Besides, it's my car, and no one else is allowed to drive it." A triumphant grin spread across his face.

I threw my hands up in the air in defeat. This was going to end terribly. I could feel it. But Summer was right—we needed to leave *now* in order to meet the deadline.

One thing we'd forgotten while we discussed our plan was Mr. Sam's bodyguards. They both stood by the boat, watching us intently. Summer caught my gaze and looked over there as well. My stomach somersaulted—I didn't like the glint in her eye.

"Hey boys," Summer called as she sauntered over to them. "I did the dumbest thing ever, you wouldn't believe." I watched as she smiled flirtatiously and adjusted her T-shirt, so her cleavage was on full display.

The men, for their part, looked more interested in what was under her shirt than what words were coming out of her mouth. One moved closer to her, and I fought the instinct to stand in front of her.

"She gripped one of them by the arm and ran her finger up and down while she giggled and squeezed his biceps. My blood pressure rose thirty points just watching this display.

The man smiled down at her, preening. "What you need from us pretty lady?" I was surprised he didn't sit up and beg with his tongue hanging out like that.

"Well, I left my undergarments on the boat, and I feel completely indecent right now. My friend Albert over there," she gestured to Albert who waved at them from where he stood, "is going to give me a ride to go pick up some clothes, but my favorite panties are still on the boat. Would it be too much trouble to have you just zoom back over to the boat really quick and grab them for me? I'd be sooo grateful!" she said, leaning even closer so they could look down her shirt. By this point, both men were practically drooling, and I had to give her props. She knew how to work it.

"Of course, Miss. We'll be right back with them." They turned to run back to the tender, tripping over lines and almost landing in the harbor as they tried to get into the boat as quickly as possible.

As soon as they were out of sight, Summer turned toward me. "Let's go."

Albert and Summer sat up front, which left Elliot and I in the back seat with Salem. Salem growled low in her throat in the carrier next to me until I pushed her over to Elliot.

"Why does that cat hate me so much?" I questioned out loud, not really expecting an answer.

"Your vibe, man. You're tense and wound tight. Also, she probably can tell you're popo. Cats don't like popo any more than the rest of us." Elliot told me.

"Maybe it's because you don't like cats," Summer called from the front seat.

It wasn't that I didn't like cats, necessarily. I just had never been around cats since my mom was allergic. The only cats I'd ever even seen other than at friends' houses were the stray cats that haunted the shopping centers and harbors on the island.

"I don't *not* like them," I grumbled, my tone whiny.

"Cats are great pets. They're much cleaner than dogs, and they aren't nearly as high maintenance," Elliot chimed in.

Before we could get into a debate over the virtues of cats versus dogs, Summer announced, "We're here."

Albert drove past the parking lot and found a pull-off a little farther down to tuck his car into. Four sets of eyes looked up at me in question.

Summer jumped out and started creeping toward the parking lot, whispering over her shoulder, "Stay here, I got this."

I just shook my head at the bullheaded woman in front of me, realizing she was likely going to be the death of me, and followed behind her, cursing under my breath.

Just as she came even with the parking lot, we heard tires crunching over gravel and the steady, low purr of a Mercedes. She stopped and motioned me to get back. I refused, and we both peered through the bushes as two men jumped out.

The men, six foot five at least, and dressed in black suits, glanced around the parking lot and said something in Russian to each other. The sound of snorting and squealing carried to us on the wind and I saw Summer's shoulders stiffen in response.

Before I could stop her, she popped out of the bushes and, once clear of our hiding spot, announced herself. "Here I am. Where's Penelope?" She strolled over to the men as if she didn't have a care in the world.

"Where is pendant?" The taller, more built of the two retorted in a heavy Russian accent.

"I don't have it on me. You can't possibly think I'd be stupid enough to bring it with me, right? That's my insurance policy. Give me Penelope and I'll tell you where the pendant is."

The man shook his head forcefully. "Nyet. Pendant, then pig."

Summer dug in her heels and argued back. "Not a chance. Give me the pig." She stepped closer as the sounds of Penelope whimpering grew louder. The second she was close enough, the other man, who'd been silent and still throughout the exchange grabbed Summer, punched her squarely in the jaw, and threw her in the car. He threw Penelope out, and she landed with a thud and a moan. Before I could even react, the men drove out of the parking lot, tires spinning and leaving a rooster tail of gravel in their wake.

I raced after the car, watching until it drove out of sight, heading south. I roared in frustration, hands on my thighs as I leaned over to catch my breath, berating myself for not stopping them somehow.

Albert and Elliot pulled up in a cloud of dust and dirt and flung the door open. Albert hopped out and tenderly lifted Penelope into the car, and I hopped in after them. We watched in the distance as the dark green Mercedes SUV turned into the driveway toward the harbor. Albert hit the gas, and my head flung back against the seat as the well-built engine highlighted all the pros of American steel, its throaty roar vibrating through me.

As we turned the corner on two wheels, all of us sliding into each other, Albert slowed the car suddenly, and we watched the Mercedes pull right up to an old navy rescue boat. The men hopped out and threw a limp Summer into it, the captain speeding away as soon as her body hit the deck.

Elliot sobbed Summer's name as we watched. The man who'd thrown Summer into the car spoke into the watch at his wrist. We crept over to him, and I leaped on top of him and wrestled him to the ground. We grappled, evenly matched in size and strength. I thought I heard a scream and when I looked up, I felt a kick to the head and then nothing.

Chapter Forty Five
SUMMER

My head pounded as I felt my body being carried, the bouncing and swaying roiled my stomach. In the distance I could hear the mournful sound of the barge horn as it headed out of port, along with the waves lapping against the shore.

Hands gripped me and I felt myself being transferred onto a boat, the gentle sway making bile rise up. Someone dropped me onto a hard surface, and I heard the murmur of male voices speaking in what I could only assume was Russian.

Vibrations from the boat motor rolled through me, the smell of diesel pushing me over the edge as I retched inside the hood covering my head. Cruel laughter followed my retching, and I kicked out in the general direction of the sound.

Stars floated above my already throbbing head as a hand smacked me above my left ear, causing me to fall back onto the hard floor again.

How long I lay there, I couldn't tell you. I winked in and out of consciousness, the powerful boat jumping waves while my head and body bounced up and down. The times I was unconscious were a blessed relief from the pain and nausea.

At some point, the boat stopped, and hands lifted me up into what I could only guess was a larger vessel, if the noise and movement were any indication.

The next thing I remembered was coming to on a luxuriously soft couch, the hood removed from my head but a gag now in place over my mouth. I cracked one eye open slowly, the light causing a stabbing pain in my head. Carefully, I looked around at my surroundings.

Inside the cabin, gold and glass elements came together to give the space an expensive, yet overdone feel. Old, expensive artifacts were showcased in little nooks throughout the cabin. I counted only one entry in and out of the space, and several cabin windows too small for anyone to fit through.

Different from Mr. Sam's yacht, this one had gaudy golden accents covering every available surface, the Gilded age but on steroids. I gazed around, wondering how much blood money went into paying for this spectacle of a boat. fleetingly, I wondered if I'd be the next casualty.

Before I had time to follow that line of thought, the door opened and in walked Demyan. He looked me over, almost clinically, his eyes cold as he watched me for any reaction. When I gave him nothing but a poker face, he shrugged his shoulders elegantly and turned to pour himself a drink from a crystal decanter filled with an amber liquid that sat on the table to his left.

He swirled the liquid, seeming to examine it before taking a sip. He turned to face me, a speculative look in his eye.

"Where is it? I am done playing these games with you." His voice would almost be pleasant, if it weren't for the undercurrent of threat that threaded through it.

I shook my head and shrugged my shoulders, unable to answer around the gag. He leaned over, close enough for me to smell whiskey on his breath, revulsion washing over me, my stomach bubbling in protest.

"No more games."

He yanked the gag down around my neck and ruthlessly gripped my hands as I tried to wipe the sting away. I gulped in a deep breath of fresh air before I answered, my head pounding like a heavy metal drummer on coke. I tried to clear my head through the noise before answering.

"What?" I eventually responded, earning me another slap on the side of the head, my head to ricocheting off the back of the couch. Nausea swamped me and I emptied my stomach onto Demyan's very expensive-looking leather loafers, which I took grim satisfaction in even as I berated myself for being a smartass at the worst times.

I wiped my mouth on the sleeve of my shirt. "Why do you want the pendant so bad?" I asked, curious.

He sneered at me, his face twisting into a mask of rage. "You don't understand the power it holds. I grew up in the communist bloc, watching men and women die of starvation as they waited in breadlines for scraps. My mother Olga, beaten down from life and trading her body for crumbs. As a child I learned the importance of power and money—and as you can see," he gestured to the cabin, filled with priceless objects and shining gold accents on every surface, "I am a very good student."

I cocked my head in confusion. "But you're already crazy rich. Why do you need the pendant?"

"Fool. There is never enough money or power."

A commotion at the door drew his attention. His shoes slopped red-stained vomit onto the plush white carpeting. Two men dressed in suits opened the door and shoved a hood covered body, arms tied behind him, inside. I knew those jeans and that backside. *Cole.*

As I watched, he tripped through the doorway, landing face first on the carpet, and I winced as his face made impact. He lay inert for several heart-stopping moments before he groaned and rolled to his back.

The two men grabbed him roughly under the shoulders and tossed him onto the seat next to me. The warmth of his body brought me comfort, but Demyan's next words crushed any sense of comfort I felt.

"I'll ask again. If your answer doesn't satisfy me, *he* will pay the price," he said, nodding his head in Cole's direction. My heart seized up as Demyan took a deadly-looking mace, testing its weight in his hand as he casually swung it around.

"One more time—Where. Is. It?"

Chapter Forty Six
COLE

Summer's body tensed next to mine, and I heard her quick intake of air and the slow hiss as she let it out. My head pounded, the black hood covering me causing near claustrophobia as I fought to remain calm. Suddenly, the hood was yanked off of me, the bright lights sending crystal shards of icepick pain to my head.

Demyan stood in front of me, swinging an ancient mace around, inching ever closer with a smile of pure evil as he watched Summer. My heartbeat skyrocketed as I watched the mace swing so close to Summer's face that the wind from it blew her hair back.

Pandemonium broke out in the hallway and brought a pause to Demyan's machinations. Crashes and shouts echoed from the hallway. With an exasperated sigh and an eye roll, he called out in Russian. The door burst open, and Elliot, Albert, Salem, and Penelope were all shoved through the door, Salem's growls and Penelope's squeals adding a surreal quality to the moment.

More Russian words passed between the two guards and Demyan. Demyan waved his arms around, his tone low and angry, while the guards pointed toward Elliot and Albert. Salem let out a wild yowl and leaped from Elliot's hands directly onto the face of the large guard to Demyan's right. Salem fought like a little kitty banshee, seemingly everywhere at once, a whirling dervish of teeth, nails, and attitude.

Furtive movement behind the other guard caught my eye, and when I looked closer, I saw the silhouette of a petite woman creep up behind the other guard and smash him over the head with a wicked-looking mallet. I swallowed hard as the mallet made contact, a hollow thunk echoing as the man dropped like a ton of bricks.

Demyan turned to the woman, the mace still in his hand, swinging it wildly in her direction, nearly taking out his own man as Salem continued her attack. He crossed toward her, inches from where I sat on the couch. As soon as his back was to me, I leaped on him and wrestled him down to the ground, the mace flying from his hand and across the floor.

My hands, still tied behind my back, handicapped me enough that I was only partially effective. He quickly gained the upper hand and flipped me on my back, his size twelve loafer moving towards my head when Summer leaped on his back, pulling his hair with one arm and wrapping her other around his windpipe in a vicious chokehold. He swung around wildly with her on his back, crashing into priceless artwork and vases as he tried to slam her against the wall.

Lani, I'd recognized her immediately from the pictures in Summer's condo, helped me to my feet. I surveyed the room; Salem, still attacking the guard, had help from Elliot and Albert, who smacked him over the head with their shoes anytime he moved within range. Penelope danced around, snorting and twirling her tail like a Kohala windmill.

Lani grimly pointed to herself and the guard, and then to me and Demyan, and I nodded in perfect understanding. I rushed across the room just as Demyan crashed into the corner, and I watched helplessly as Summer's head snapped back with a thud as it crashed into a metal gong. She slipped down, unconscious, as the gong continued to vibrate.

By now, Demyan was foaming at the mouth and didn't even come close to resembling the polished European man I'd met at the harbor several days ago. The deranged look on his face and unholy light in his eyes clued me in—this would be a fight to the death.

I charged him, taking him out at the knees, but at the last second, he twisted, landing on top of me and jabbing his elbow into my trachea. Air whistled as I tried to drag in a breath. Demyan grabbed a deadly-looking Maka Pahoa, a double-edged knife, from a hidden cabinet to his left, and began swinging it around in a figure-eight pattern, advancing on me with intent.

I struggled to gain my footing, still seeing stars as he closed in. From out of nowhere, a black flash flew past me and attached itself to Demyan's face. He reached across with his empty hand and tore Salem off of him and then threw her against the wall, as she screeched and then lay still.

With a cry of fury, Elliot raced across the room, outrage plain on his face as he wielded his slipper. Demyan, unimpressed, smacked the slipper out of Elliot's hand and moved to grab his hair, but I swept his legs and he crashed to the floor. I pounced on him, kicking like the Kansas City Chiefs in the fourth quarter of the Super Bowl while Elliot hit him from the other side with his shoe. Even Salem jumped in, recovered from her flight across the room, sinking her teeth and nails into any exposed flesh.

I risked a glance over at Lani just as she smashed the guard right in the nuts and watched as he toppled over like a Redwood in fire season. As I watched, she leaped in the air, and did a flying Diving Double Axe Handle like Randy Savage from the WWE. The crunch as she made contact made even me wince. She shifted her eyes at me and winked.

Demyan was slowly coming around, pushing Elliot off of him and trying to get a hold of Salem. I kicked Demyan in the head just as the door burst open to a flood of navy-blue uniforms, guns drawn.

"Freeze!" came a voice from behind the officers, and I watched in astonishment as Salem froze momentarily before sitting and licking her paw as if nothing had happened. I rolled my eyes just as the Chief turned the corner into the room; I gave Demyan one last solid kick before dropping to my knees next to Summer, her body unnaturally still.

Chapter Forty Seven

COLE

I HELD SUMMER IN my arms, Elliot and Lani flanking me, as we waited for the paramedics to make their way onto the boat. Albert sat on the overstuffed chair next to Lani, holding Salem and Penelope in his lap. He murmured words of praise to both of them for their bravery. At one point he looked over at me and said, "Salem's a good name for this brave little guy."

"Guy? What do you mean? I thought Salem was a girl—" I shook my head, mystified.

He chuckled and then carefully lifted Salem's tail, so I could see that Salem was definitely a boy and wasn't neutered. Summer chuckled, amusement washing over her. She winced when she tried to turn her head and look at Salem, and I told her to keep still. A slight frown of irritation crossed her face. "Don't be bossy," she said, but kept her head still and her eyes closed after that.

We watched as Demyan and his goons were hauled away, Demyan's parting words, "You'll regret crossing me," thrown over his shoulder at me, his stare penetrating. I shrugged my shoulders. So be it. For now, Summer was safe, Wainright's murderer was in custody, and as I looked around at the motley cast of characters surrounding me, I couldn't help but think how fortunate I was to have found them.

Elliot grinned at me, and I matched the grin as I looked down at Summer, then over at Albert, who mirrored Elliot. Finally, I looked at Lani and she smiled up at me, a twinkle of mischief in her expression.

"So, you're the famous Lani," I said. "Nice to finally meet you." I reached over to shake her hand, and she gazed first at my hand, then back up at my face before shaking my hand, her grip stronger than most men.

"And you're the famous Detective Daddy," she replied, earning a pinch and a grimace from Summer.

Laughter rang out, and once we started, none of us could stop. That's how Jack Hall found us, leaned up against each other, howling like lunatics.

Jack peered down at us, one eyebrow quirked, a speculative look on his face. He reached down to shake my hand.

"Great job, Cole. If it weren't for you, we never would have caught Demyan. Thanks to you, we have a solid case against him. I'd like to see him try to worm his way out of this one." His gaze landed on Summer, and he frowned.

"I'm sorry you got caught up in all of this, and especially sorry you were hurt." Summer nodded, her movements slow and deliberate. "I'll have to get your statement, but we'll hold off until after we get you checked out."

Jack pressed a button on the black earpiece in his right ear and let us know the paramedics had boarded. I nodded at him gratefully and then groaned as the Chief made his way over to us.

"Well, Peterson, you're lucky we found Demyan's boat when we did. Otherwise, you and your friends could've been killed. Once we're back at the station, we're going to have a long talk about your reckless behavior and handling of this case. If it weren't for my research into Demyan's holdings and finding his name on the company manifest for this yacht, who knows what could've happened." Chief puffed up his chest as he talked, looking like a goddamned rooster about to crow.

"Actually, Takada, I'd like to hear more about how you allowed an international arms dealer and known drug trafficker to fly under the radar here for several weeks with no surveillance. Or how, after Detective Peterson came to you with concerns about the operations of a Yakuza corporation you shut him down. And I'd also like to talk to you about the fact that you only responded to Detective Peterson's concerns *after* receiving phone calls from Honolulu ICPO. In fact, why don't we schedule a time for all of us to sit down and discuss exactly what and *who* your associations are on this island."

Chief's chest deflated and his face grew redder as Jack threw question after question at him, scalding me with a look of vicious promise. I smiled back and wiggled my fingers at him in goodbye as Jack moved him out of the way for the paramedics.

They carefully loaded Summer on to a backboard and spoke in hushed tones to her as they went about packaging her for the ride back to the harbor. Elliot, Albert, Penelope, and Salem all followed a step behind as they rolled her down the narrow hallway and to the waiting Coast Guard tender.

"Can we go with her?" Elliot asked, worry etched on his face. The paramedic pushing the stretcher, a brawny Hawaiian guy, looked around at all of us, curiosity clear in his expression.

"Normally, we wouldn't allow anyone. I'll make an exception this time though—I bet there's an interesting story to hear."

Elliot, Lani, and I volunteered and jostled to go, but Jack called my name and yelled, "Hey, I need to get your statement."

I protested, but then looked at Elliot and Lani, love and apprehension for Summer radiating off them, and bowed out gracefully, leaning down to kiss Summer softly before stepping away. I watched as they got Summer situated in the tender, Elliot and Lani bickering their way into a spot on the boat. I shook my head and laughed, relief washing over me.

Jack motioned me over and we discussed the events leading up to Summer's kidnapping. As we talked, we made our way to the back of the yacht where a gaudy, Liberace-esque sparkly purple Nitro bass boat was tied up. Jack stood in front, looking anywhere but at me when I asked him who's boat it was.

He hemmed and hawed before answering, "Mine." His voice was so quiet I almost didn't hear him. I gazed in disbelief at Jack and then at the boat, and then back to Jack before bursting into laughter.

"Oh my God, I can't wait to tell everyone at the station!" I said, hunched over and holding my stomach in between laughing fits.

"Yeah, yeah, tough guy, but if you want to get to the harbor, you're going to have to ride in it."

I stood up abruptly, opening my mouth in horror as I looked at the monstrosity on the water. Jack put his arm on my shoulder.

"Unless you want to wait hours until HPD is ready to go, that is. But I bet that pretty girl headed to the hospital probably wants to see your ugly mug sooner." He shook his head in mock dismay. "There's just no accounting for taste," he said sadly.

I snorted. "Look who's talking," I said, and we both turned to gaze down, the sun reflecting on the boat, making it appear to glow neon purple.

Jack filled me in on what happened after I texted him, right before Demyan's goons grabbed me as we made our way back to the harbor. It seems the FBI and HPD were already looking into who owned the yacht, considering the timing suspicious on when it appeared off the Kohala Coast. After sifting through countless shell corporations, they found Demyan's name listed on the manifest as a board member. The judge signed the warrant immediately and the FBI called in the Coast Guard.

"So how'd you end up taking this sweet ride out to Demyan's vessel?" I teased.

"I was already out running surveillance, posing as a fisherman, making passes as close as I dared when I saw their tender race out here then back twice more. I knew something must have happened, because you weren't responding to my texts."

I nodded, for the first time taking in the fishing poles positioned in their rod holders and the bucket of bait near the stern of the boat. I raised my eyes to Jack.

"Dude. You were fishing when you got my text?"

Jack smiled, unrepentant, as he pulled up to the dock. I hopped out and tied lines, nearly toppling into the water as a wave of dizziness hit. Jack noticed and raised an eyebrow.

"Summer's not the only one who took a hit, I'm guessing," he probed.

I shook my head. "I'm fine, let's get that paperwork done so I can go get my girl."

Chapter Forty Eight

SUMMER

SOMEONE SHINED A BRIGHT light into my eye, peeling my eyelid up because I refused to open them.

"Ahhh!" I moaned, the light sending piercing pain to my head. My arms were strapped down to the hard gurney underneath me, so I couldn't even swipe at the monster with the penlight.

"Sorry Summer. I just have to check your pupils," a disembodied voice murmured, a Hawaiian accent coloring his words. I nodded, or at least I think I did.

"It's okay. Just hurts," I muttered.

Although I didn't dare open my eyes, I felt Elliot and Lani pressed in near me on the boat. Lani held my hand on one side while Elliot rubbed my arm carefully on the other.

Snippets and flashes of my struggle with Demyan and the mayhem that occurred on the boat ran through my head as Elliot and Lani told the story to the paramedics. I heard them chuckle when Elliot told them about Penelope and Salem. I cracked a smile too—I mean, how ludicrous is it to think that we owe a large part of our success, and likely our lives to one pissed off cat?

"Sounds like the cat deserves treats for life after all of that," the paramedic said, his voice fluid and deep. I murmured my agreement along with everyone else.

"Wait!" I cried, and I felt everyone tense up. "Where's Albert and the animals?" I knew Cole needed to stay behind and fill out reports, but it just occurred to me I didn't know what happened to Albert.

Lani rubbed my hand with her thumb soothingly as she answered, "He's fine. HPD was going to give him a ride back after they took his statement." I relaxed, knowing that our ragtag crew had all made it through our ordeal safely.

Once onshore, the paramedics loaded me into the waiting ambulance, and Elliot and Lani said they'd meet me at the hospital.

"How are you getting up there?" I asked.

I cracked my left eye open and watched as Lani's face morphed into an evil grin as she pointed to Auntie Miriam's custom Cadillac. I gasped and Lani laughed, "Don't worry, once she hears the story, she'll forgive me."

Oh, what I wouldn't give to be a fly on the wall for that conversation. I waved goodbye and politely asked the paramedics to turn off the screaming siren before I broke it. The older one shrugged his shoulder and the infernal noise stopped.

They admitted me for observation at Queens. I tried to fight it, I just wanted to go home and sleep. The doctor was kind but firm when he told me I needed to stay, that they had diagnosed me as having a moderate concussion and wanted to keep an eye on me overnight. Eventually I gave in, mostly because the pounding headache made talking and thinking hard.

Elliot came in to see me first, a giant whale plushy in his arms. I smiled at him. "Is that for me?"

He hugged it close to himself. "No."

I laughed at him, and he smiled before placing it next to me in the bed. "I'm so glad you're okay," he whispered. Even though I could tell he was doing his best, his red-rimmed eyes and raw voice gave him away. I cupped his face and looked into his eyes.

"You saved me. You and Albert and Lani and Cole. You guys saved me." My voice hitched at the end, and even though I was doing my best to hold it together, a tear rolled down my cheek.

Elliot wiped it away and kissed my forehead gently. "And don't think I'm not going to remind you of that for the next forty years or so," he said, causing me to giggle. "Get some rest. We'll be nearby if you need us."

I nodded and drifted off, only to wake up when I smelled Lani's signature perfume, a scent that reminded me of the ocean and fresh breezes, the only nod to femininity she allowed herself. I opened my eyes and saw her sitting in a folding chair next to my bed, staring down at her hands.

"Hey," I said.

"Hey," she replied, her voice thick with emotion and eyes glistening with tears.

"Did you give Auntie her car back yet?" I asked, dying of curiosity.

Lani shifted in her seat and shook her head no. "She's on her way up here though," Lani said, her voice tinged with dread.

"Well, at least I'm off the hook. She can't get mad at someone in a hospital bed."

Lani snorted. "Wanna bet?"

Shit. Lani watched my face closely as dismay and apprehension surged through me. She patted my hand.

"If it's any consolation, I'm sure I'll wear her out first." We shared a smile and then she tipped her forehead to mind and took in a deep breath. I could feel all the tension coiled in her body slowly release.

"Lani. How did you get to the boat so fast?" It had just occurred to me that Lani showed up just in time—but how?

"I never left the island." My eyes widened in disbelief. Before I could pester her for answers, she continued. "I needed you, and especially Demyan and his men, to think I'd left. I sent half his team on a merry chase across part of the Southwest and Colorado over the last few days—" she said, a satisfied grin on her face.

"Explain," I demanded.

She heaved a sigh and settled into her chair. "After you got run off the road, I realized whoever was behind Wainright's murder was going to keep coming after you. Partly because of me, and partly because you discovered the body. Whoever had the pendant needed the Lei o mano in order to complete the set. I left breadcrumbs of clues for them to follow to take the heat off of you. When they kept coming, I decided to make them think I'd run to the mainland."

I shook my head in amazement. Lani was born in the wrong era. She should've been running her own army, or captaining a pirate ship or something.

"So anyway, I bought a one-way ticket to Las Vegas, pretended to get on the plane, and then set up a series of rental cars and itineraries in my name for them to chase." She swiped a hand over her face, and I noticed something I hadn't earlier. Lani looked exhausted.

"Instead of traipsing about the mainland, I actually started following leads and figured out it was Demyan who killed Wainright." She smiled widely. "I saw you at the Fairmont in your coconut bra. I even snapped some pictures to spread on the internet if you ever mess with me." I laughed, knowing she never would.

"After Auntie got ahold of the pendant and told me what happened, I figured it was just a matter of time before Demyan went after you. I just didn't think you'd be dumb enough to meet with them like that."

My shoulders sagged in embarrassment, but her next words surprised me. "Seems like something I would've done." Her smile took the sting out of her earlier words.

Just then, Auntie and Mr. Sam walked in. Lani immediately tensed and I straightened up in my bed, moving so fast I winced from the jarring in my head. Auntie's severe look softened before she turned her eyes on Lani and said, "Hallway."

As I watched, Lani, the second toughest person I knew, drug her feet across the floor and was the closest to afraid I'd ever seen, making her way out of the room at turtle speed.

Mr. Sam and I watched, a bemused smile playing on his face. He turned to me and I held my hands up. "Before you say anything, I just want to say I'm sorry for fooling your guys and taking off like that. I know it was stupid. There were extenuating circumstances, but that doesn't excuse me from abusing your hospitality like that."

Silence reigned for a full, excruciating minute before he nodded in acknowledgement. "There's an old Japanese saying that roughly translates to 'you have a healthy dose of curiosity and a miserly amount of self-preservation'."

Ouch. I couldn't disagree though, and instead I bowed my head and nodded. He reached over and cupped my chin, his touch gentle. "I admire your warrior heart and desire to save your friends."

His words touched something deep inside that needed to hear that. I nodded as a tear welled up and spilled over. Mr. Sam perused me for a moment before saying, "You remind me of my daughter. Headstrong and impetuous, but a fierce protector of her loved ones." His voice was gruff, emotion thick underneath. "You will have my protection from here on out." And with that, he turned on his heel and left before I could protest or even ask what that meant.

Cole was next. He came in carrying a giant bouquet, anthuriums, birds of paradise, proteas, and orchids all vying for dominance, Cole's face barely visible behind them.

My eyes followed him as he set them down on the counter underneath the TV, fussing with the placement for a moment before drawing in a deep breath and turning towards me.

His eyes took in everything, and I watched as he swallowed when he saw the bandage on my head.

"It's not as bad as it looks," I told him.

He didn't look convinced, and I held out my hand to reassure him. His eyes locked onto our joined hands, and I saw his chest heave. I squeezed, and he closed his eyes and drew in a deep breath.

"Hey, I'm okay, really. I promise. The doctor just wanted to keep me for observation."

He bowed his head for a moment and then nodded before looking into my eyes, finally. I saw as the muscles in his jaw clenched then released. Oh so gently he smoothed my hair and kissed me on the lips, so tender for such a big guy.

"I'm taking you out on a proper date. Flowers, candlelight, white tablecloth, the whole nine yards. Just you and me."

Not where I was expecting this to go, but I agreed with a haste that should've embarrassed me, nodding so eagerly in anticipation that the room started to spin.

A knock at the door interrupted the goofy smile we shared and in walked my mom. I made introductions and I watched as my mom eyed Cole up and down, female appreciation obvious in her glance and the subtle thumbs up she gave me. Well, not so subtle, judging by the way Cole's grin widened as he waved goodbye with the promise to check on me a little later.

Mom fussed over me as only moms do, but before she could pull out her healing crystals and essential oils, I faked a yawn, which she noticed immediately. Tucking the covers in around me she kissed my cheek and told me to rest.

I'd just closed my eyes when I heard a commotion in the hallway. A voice that sounded like my mom's, and a lower-pitched one. It sounded like arguing, but I couldn't quite make out the words.

"Fine!" I heard clearly, my mom's voice ringing out, right before my door opened and a large man, his sandy hair shaped into a crew cut, and shoulders like a linebacker walked in.

"Dad!" I said, surprise causing me to sit up straight in bed. My dad hadn't set foot in Hawaii in I don't even know how many years, yet here he was.

"Hey, Pumpkin. I hear you found some adventure." He walked over and hugged me, his solid warmth reminded me of my childhood and how he always picked me up when I fell. Tears I didn't even know I had in me fell.

Once I got control of myself, I asked what he was doing here.

"Well, funny you should ask. I was already on a plane on my way here when I got a frantic text from your mom."

"You were already on your way?" I asked, confused.

He nodded. "Remember when we talked last week about the business and how I wanted you to join me as a partner?" I nodded, wary.

"Well, the more I thought about it, the more I realized that other than the business, there's really nothing holding me to Arizona any longer. Now that I'm getting older, I'd like to pass on my legacy to you, but since you won't move back to Arizona, maybe I need to come to you."

It took me a minute for my addled brain to process his words. Growing apprehension filled me. He couldn't mean? There's no way he would even consider? Would he? Dread climbed up, digging its sharp little hooks in my throat.

His next words crashed over me, and not to be too dramatic, but life as I knew it changed forever.

"I'm moving to the Big Island and opening up my own PI business here. TS Jenkins Investigations. Get it? T for Thomas and S for Summer..."

Epilogue

LANI

ENTRANCED BY THE ARTIFACT in front of me, I almost missed Auntie Miriam's words. The azure blue stone in the middle seemed to almost light up from inside, the color swirling from light to dark as if it were alive. Faint buzzing filled my ears, and the pendant invited me closer, a whisper of energy pulling my hand down to the satin-lined box where it lay as my heart thudded in anticipation.

Just before my fingers could caress it, Auntie Miriam slammed the box shut with a resounding thud, and it took me a moment to emerge from the spell. She tipped my chin up to look into her eyes.

"You understand now why we must protect the pendant? In the wrong hands chaos would result."

I nodded; a part of my brain still caught up in the visions the pendant evoked. I shook my head to dispel the visions.

Auntie watched me, a strange stillness surrounding us. Her eyes took in every expression on my face, and I shivered as I wondered if she was reading my mind at the same time.

"The mana is strong. We must protect this pendant and keep it away from all who may covet it for their own wicked purposes. The world as we know it could forever be changed if the pendant fell into the wrong hands."

"I thought it only worked if the Lei o mano was also present?" I asked.

She shook her head grimly. Her finger caressed the box in front of her and she seemed a thousand miles away, lost in her own thoughts.

She pulled herself out of her reverie, and when she noticed the way her hand lay on the box in front of her, she snatched it away and took in a deep breath before letting it out slowly.

Shivering, I looked around as the damp night air settled over me. Auntie had insisted we meet in secret, even ordering me to park a mile away and hike to the cliffs overlooking the ocean. The ironwood trees blotted out the sliver of moon above our heads, making the trail even more difficult to follow. Five hundred feet below us, the surf crashed against the volcanic rock butting up against the cliffs. Chicken skin rose on my bare arms, and the thrum of the Earth vibrated through me.

"Auntie?" I spoke, hating the wobble in my voice.

"The pendant carries powerful mana of its own. Throughout its history many people have died, and lives were torn apart to possess it. When it was created, the intent was to imbue it with enough power to unite the islands and stop the wars and bloodshed. As its legend grew, so did the desire to control it."

She turned to me, her normally twinkling hazel eyes almost opaque, and her voice sounded different with the words that followed.

"We must return it back to its birthplace, Lani. She is tired and wants to rest."

"What do you mean? What birthplace? And how do you know it wants to rest?"

When Auntie looked at me next, the opaque layer had dissipated, but her expression was somber. "It told me."

She handed me the box and motioned to the raging sea below.

Acknowledgements

This book series is my quirky little love letter to the Big Island. A lot of the places I've mentioned are real places, slightly adjusted at times to fit the story. For reasons unknown to me this island and the people in it have accepted me, and this is my way to pay homage to this beautiful little corner of the world!

I'd also like to say thank you to the real-life characters that inspired my book. You know who you are–and I hope you smiled as you read the book!

To my book bestie, my soul sister, my OG hype girl Jessica Belshe. You kept me going in so many ways. Your support, encouragement, practical advice, and IG technical talent gave me the courage I needed to go for it. Thank you doesn't even begin to cover it but thank you! And I'm definitely paying for dinner in Hawaii!

Thank you to my editor Heather Osborn– I'm sorry, Heather, Pat Morita had to stay!

To my amazing husband who supports and encourages me– thank you! And thank you for the practical suggestions that make the male characters more realistic!

Lastly, thank you to all the people who chose to read this book. I hope you enjoyed it and maybe even laughed a few times... Your support means everything to me!

About the author

Christine Wellert is a writer, mother of 3 humans and several canines, wife to her high school sweetheart, Registered Nurse, and author of the Barefoot Sleuth Cozy Mysteries set on the Big Island of Hawaii.

While Christine has spent most of her adult life working in the medical field, her true passion and love (aside from her family and friends) is reading, writing, and drinking coffee (and not always in that order...). Interested in all things metaphysical and woowoo, she weaves aspects of those into her all of her stories.

Christine studied creative writing in college and enjoys creating characters and stories that encourage and empower readers.

Christine splits her time between the Pacific Northwest and Hawaii. When not chained to her keyboard, you can find Christine hiking, skiing, scuba diving, or traveling.

IF YOU'D LIKE TO CHAT YOU CAN FIND ME ON THE LINKS BELOW, OR SCAN THE QR CODE TO GO DIRECTLY TO MY WEBSITE:

Instagram- @christinewellertauthor
Facebook- christinewellertauthor
TikTok- @christinewellertauthor
Website- www.ChristineWellert.com

And if you liked the book and really want to help a sister out, I would be so thankful (and maybe even send you homemade cookies) if you could write a review on Goo dreads.com, Bookbub, Amazon, or wherever you typically leave reviews. This really helps get my book in front of more people so they can share in the zany fun!
https://www.amazon.com/review/create-review?&asin=B0G27LMY2G